"I love reading Georg[e ...]ly funny."

"Every George Baxt bo[...] D.W. Griffith movie, with th[e ...]hat Griffith, who had little sense of humor, would not have planted so many explosive one-liners and verbal pratfalls along the way. Baxt's final chapters tend to provoke alternating gasps of surprise and whoops of hysterical laughter from his readers."

— Michael Feingold
Village Voice

"One of the finest of modern satirists."

— Jeff Banks
Twentieth Century Crime and Mystery Writers

GEORGE BAXT

THE NEON GRAVEYARD

A CRIME CLASSIC ®

INTERNATIONAL POLYGONICS, LTD.
NEW YORK CITY

This book is for
Steven Dansky and Bret Adams
and special guest star,
Leonard Soloway

1

Young man, I think you've had it.

It was the first time he admitted defeat to himself. It was the first time he'd ever felt this tired, this beaten, this bloodied. He leaned against the grillwork door gasping for breath, wondering what to do next. His right eye was painfully swollen, and the left one was curtained with blood oozing from his lacerated eyebrow. He leaned forward and shook his head and saw drops of blood dapple the flagstones at his feet. The fierce wind blowing at this height did everything but scatter the confusion in his mind. His thought processes were becoming as unreliable as a fair-weather friend. He knew he had been doped.

He could feel the dampness of the fog rolling in from the Pacific and wished someone had the decency to bring the condemned man an extremely dry vodka martini on the rocks. He wiped his left eye with his tuxedo sleeve and brought into focus the Hollywood hills with their twinkling lights, a whore wearing sequins. How many hundreds of feet up am I, he wondered. His jacket and trousers were soiled and torn, and it annoyed him. He was a fastidious man. He was glad he wouldn't have to explain the condition of the suit and backed away slowly, trembling. He faced her and said with a controlled voice, "You'll catch cold up here."

"You'll catch worse for this," she said with a weak voice. "You will, you know. He won't like this. He won't like this at all. There was to be no violence here. He promised me that. It was part of our deal."

"It wasn't part of mine." He jerked his head toward the void that had been briefly filled by the doomed young man. "He could have finished us."

"You didn't have to kill him here!" Her voice had regained its strength, and he recognized the fire in her eyes. "The boys could have handled him. They know how to do these things."

"He saw me. He would have finished me."

"You didn't have to kill him here! We could have locked him up in the dungeon until the boys got back from Vegas. Oh, you are so tiresome!" She turned on her heel and clattered toward the grillwork door. There she turned and watched him struggling to light a cigarette in the fierce wind. "You don't even have the sense to do *that* indoors."

"You know there's only one thing I like to do indoors."

"You bungle that too." She turned and disappeared. He listened to the clatter of her heels on the stone stairs and then crumpled the cigarette in a beefy fist and sent it flying after the doomed young man.

The morning sun was fighting a losing battle against the smog blanketing Los Angeles. Detective Ira Sparks wiped his eyes with a handkerchief and then stared at the corpse sprawled like an idle puppet on the grass.

"Why do they dump everything in Griffith Park?" he said with a groan to his associate, Detective Boyd Gross.

"It's so convenient," replied Gross.

The coroner, Maurice Mosk, completed the swift preliminary examination of the corpse. "He's got an awful lot of broken bones. That's quite a beating he took. I'm sure he didn't die here."

Norton thought she expected a blare of trumpets. He smiled what his friends would call his practiced dumb smile. The lady leaned toward him as though to offer a challenge.

"Lila *Frank*."

"How do you do, Miss Frank," he said affably. "I'm Norton Valentine."

"Don't you *read* me?"

"Quite easily. I see a lovely brunette with beautiful skin, hazel eyes, full red lips . . ."

"You mean you never *heard* of me?" Everything about the lady was lovely except her voice. It was shrill and strident and should have been quoting a bargain in fish. "'Frankly Speaking'."

"Go right ahead. If anything I've said has offended you . . ."

"It's what you *haven't* said that's offended me, you boob." Then she wrinkled her nose and smiled. "You're pulling my leg."

"Later, if you're free."

"You *really* haven't heard of me." She spoke to the ceiling. "Syndicated in over two hundred papers across the world, a weekly television spot, and he hasn't heard of me. Well, so much for the power of the media." She examined his face. "Where you been living the past three years? Tibet?"

Norton leaned toward her cozily. "I don't read tabloids. I don't read gossip columns. I'm a stockbroker."

"Okay, Norton. I never knock money. Got any hot tips?"

He spread five fingers.

"Save them for your wife."

"I'm not married."

The film ended, and shades were raised, and the cabin brightened with sunlight. Lila pulled the zipper on her manicure case and tucked it into her alligator handbag. It gave her time to digest Norton Valentine. Probably in his mid-thirties with rugged good looks, traces of gray around his temples and even white teeth, and when he stood up, she was sure his frame would straighten into a lithe, lean, well-proportioned body. Some girl might strike it lucky tonight, if

Leigh, the enchanting tigress photographers fought to immortalize in celluloid. Marti Leigh, of whom one powerful advertising executive had said, "She could convince the great unwashed to brush their teeth with lye." Marti Leigh, whose eyes signaled Yes and whose lips could never say No. Marti Leigh, the cuddlesome bunny with morals to match.

Norton's film of memory screened an incident that had occurred four years before. He had met, pursued, wooed and won the glamorous Marti. The honeymoon in Nassau had been so idyllic, Norton considered selling the film rights. In Washington, D.C., Clay Stopley, Norton's closest friend and business associate gave the blissful newlyweds a dinner party. Marti was the center of attraction, and Norton stood to one side with Clay, admiring his glorious bride.

"She's too beautiful," commented Clay with admiration. "A wife like that would give me insomnia."

"Who sleeps?"

Clay looked at Norton with envy. "I suppose she's giving up her career to be housewife and mother. Another fallen sparrow."

"We haven't discussed it. She still has contracts to fulfill."

"If she was mine, I wouldn't let her out of my sight."

"I don't have your insecurities, kid. She can do anything that keeps her happy."

And Marti did everything that kept her happy, including a Republican senator, a halfback with the Green Bay Packers and Clay Stopley.

"Clay . . . my best friend . . . *Why?*"

Marti shrugged. "Because he was there."

The palm of Norton's hand connected with Marti's cheek. She staggered against the bedroom wall, tears stinging her eyes. She blinked rapidly and then folded her hands. "Why hit me? Hit him."

"I already have." He jerked a suitcase from the closet and tossed it on the bed. "You better see your lawyer. I've already seen mine."

"Did you hit him too?"

"Norton," said Lila blithely, "I think you're going to do just fine out here."

Norton removed his address book from his jacket breast pocket and began flipping pages. He studied some names and then asked Lila, "You probably know everybody. Who's Hagar Simon?" He glanced at her in time to see her face go rigid. "Your worst enemy?"

"What? Who? Hagar? Good Christ, no. Who gave you *her* name, of all people?"

"Friend of mine in New York. Harvey Tripp."

"Harvey Tripp," repeated Lila with mock awe. "You certainly know a lot of boys at the top."

"I get around."

"I can see you do. Didn't he tell you about Hagar?"

"Nothing much. Just that she's a great gal and throws some terrific parties. Her husband used to be a producer or something."

"Hardly 'or something.' Isaac Simon's a legend out here. Until the conglomerates squeezed him out and gave him his fatal heart attack, he was right up there on top with Sam Goldwyn and Louis B. Mayer. He created Hagar. Didn't you ever see any of her pictures?"

"Hagar *Simon?* Sorry. It doesn't ring a bell."

"Neither did she. She was Hagar Holt, the ice skater."

"Ohhhh, Hagar *Holt*. She used to be quite a dish."

"The hottest thing on ice. And still a very handsome woman." Lila examined her cuticle. "Couldn't make it as an actress, though. Poor Simon poured millions into her career, and that's what did him in with his stockbrokers. When he died five years ago, they were so broke, she was down to one cat."

"So who pays for her terrific parties?"

A wry smile appeared on Lila's face. "That's anybody's guess. Hagar's a smart lady. She managed to rise out of the ashes. I'm sure you know about her castle."

"You mean she really lives in a castle? I thought Harvey Tripp was kidding me."

and stroking the chinchilla coat at her side. She stared out the window deep in thought, the subject under consideration being Norton Valentine. Handsome. Glib. Successful. Available. A likely catch for any girl out trawling.

Why haven't I heard of him before?

Lila snapped her fingers, reached for the telephone and dialed. After three rings, she heard a whiskey-soaked voice slur, "Hello?"

She purred, "Hello, Burton, darling."

The voice at the other end brightened. "Sweetheart! When'd you get back?"

"I'm in my car right now, heading for home. New York was ghastly, but mission accomplished."

"What's the word from the old man?"

"Tell you all about it when I see you. Now Burton put down your drink . . ."

"I'm not . . ."

"Put *down* your drink, and write down this name. Norton Valentine."

"What about him?"

"Do you *know* him?"

"Never heard of him. Who is he?"

Lila gently scratched a thigh. "That's what I want you to find out. I sat next to him on the plane. Quite a dish, but I wasn't hungry. He says he's a friend of Harvey Tripp's." She could hear ice cubes dropping into a glass.

"If he is, then he's somebody."

"But what kind of a somebody? He says Harvey told him to get in touch with Hagar."

"Harvey's most discreet about that."

"Exactly. I want you to check this guy out."

"Why? Did he rub you the wrong way?"

"Not yet. But I don't know. You know my instincts."

"I know your instincts," he repeated flatly. "Harvey's a hard guy to track down, but I'll get on it right away. What's this Valentine like?" Lila gave him the full description. "I'll

2

"If I was looking for a score, I'd go for that fat redhead in the psychedelic bikini." Ira Sparks stood at the window in Norton's living room, which also looked out on the swimming pool. Norton crossed to the detective's side, while buttoning his jacket, and stared at the obese subject under discussion.

"I'd make her take a saliva test," commented Norton. Sparks moved away from the window with a grin, while Norton followed him with his eyes. "What do those girls out there do besides exhibit themselves?"

"Oh, some of them are legit. Singers here for a recording date. New York actresses in for a tee-vee spot. Actors' wives. A few hookers. The usual afternoon crowd at a hotel swimming pool. The men start putting in an appearance around five. They're the ones whose hair is longer. Which reminds me," he said, glancing at his wristwatch, "we'd better get a move on if we want to catch Maurice at the ice palace." He answered Norton's questioning look. "The morgue. The deep freeze. Maurice Mosk is our coroner." He walked slowly to the door. "Your buddy's apartment was on the other side of the pool." He shook his head. "Funny how I

Better make sure he's in a sealed coffin. We'll trump up some reason. Car crash. Something like that. I wouldn't want his folks to see him like this. He was one hell of a good looking guy."

The four adjourned to Ira Sparks's office, where they huddled over containers of coffee. Mosk had memorized the deceased's bone breaks and fractures and recited them by rote. Norton listened in stony silence.

"And that's why I think he either fell or was pushed from some elevation," concluded Mosk.

"What about his face? Could the impact of a fall have done that much damage?"

"No. They rarely land face down. That was done with a blunt instrument, like maybe a rock. Lots of rocks in Griffith Park."

Norton turned to Sparks. "Find any rock out there with blood on it?"

"No, but we're still looking. Somebody with a good pitching arm could be giving us a hard time."

"I'm not finished," interjected Mosk. "There were other bruises on the neck, shoulders and torso that indicated he had taken a beating. His knuckles were scraped, which indicates he at least attempted to put up some defense. For good measure, I did an autopsy. He'd been doped, and a fair guess is it was a pretty heavy dose."

"Alcohol?" asked Norton.

"Oh, sure there was alcohol, but not enough for a conviction if he'd been pulled in for drunk driving."

"I wish he had been," said Norton before sipping some coffee.

"Gerber's wants to know who's going to pay for the tuxedo." Boyd Gross looked almost naively cherubic.

Norton sat back in his chair. "We'll take care of it."

We, thought Gross, who's this we? Who's this Norton Valentine? Who's the stiff? Who the hell was Clay Stopley?

Sparks interrupted Gross's train of thought as he addressed Norton. "I can have Stopley's suitcase brought up. I've gone

— 15 —

"Maybe he didn't get the chance."

"I mean, just that one meeting with him at the hotel a couple of weeks ago, and that's all. I don't even know if he ever got inside Hagar's castle."

"I think he got inside," said Norton casually.

"You think, or you know?" Sparks dropped some ash on the floor with an exaggerated gesture.

"Clay was a very smart operator." He sank back in thought. He got inside, Mr. Sparks, and unless you're a big fool, and I don't think you are, you know he got inside. Just like I will get inside, either through my introduction from Harvey Tripp or through a young lady Clay was seeing here in Hollywood. Clay didn't like you, Mr. Sparks, and Clay liked just about everybody. That was his most serious shortcoming, but one overlooked that because he usually brought home the goods. *How* the hell was he tripped up, or *who* the hell did it?"

"Something you want to tell me?" asked Sparks abruptly. "I mean, whoever Clay Stopley was, it's still my murder case."

"I'm not forgetting that. But we have our orders too, you know." He favored the detective with his practiced dumb smile. "Sorry about that, but that's how it has to be."

Sparks responded with a Gallic shrug. "And I suppose now you storm the castle."

"Nothing so melodramatic. I'll be invited there. The way Clay was invited there."

Sparks crushed the cheroot in an ashtray with an angry movement. "If you know he's been there, why don't you come out with it and say so? Have you seen the place?"

"Not yet."

"It's an effing tall monstrosity, mister. It's a real honest-to-God castle. It's got turrets and stonework and ramparts, everything except the drawbridge and moat. You know how high ramparts are? Very high! A guy could get killed if he got dumped from one. Of course, it could have been an accident. Mosk tells us there was dope and alcohol in him. If he was at

— 17 —

"They could be. Viola Pickfair admitted to having met Stopley once on a double date with a friend of hers named Karen Frost."

"Was Karen Frost at the castle Monday night?"

Sparks seemed chagrined. "It didn't occur to me to find out."

"It can wait. The Pickfair girl can probably tell me how to connect with her."

"You intend to interview all these people?"

"Not all. Just the Pickfair girl to start with. After all, I'm not a detective. I'm a stockbroker in town on business. I happen to have known Clay Stopley. We were at Rutgers together. I saw an item about his death in tomorrow's paper, right?"

"It'll be in."

"So I went to the police, met you, got what few facts you know, and decided to call on Miss Pickfair. With any luck, I might even take her to dinner."

"Luck will be on your side. She's a nut. She kept asking if I'd seen her three months ago on 'Charlie's Angels,' and when I told her I never saw the program in my life, she says, what do I mean I never saw the program why just about everybody in the whole United States and Canada watches that program and what kind of a creep am I who doesn't watch a program beloved by . . . Oh, my God, I've caught it from her." He was mopping his brow with a handkerchief. "Her aunt Chloe was another unusual experience, let me tell you. What with her gorilla . . ."

"A bodyguard?"

"A bodyguard, but a *real* gorilla." Norton's eyebrows went up. "His name's Irving."

"Gorillas can crush a man to death. Even a gorilla named Irving."

"I never even thought of that. I must be slipping. Chloe Jupiter is Hagar Simon's neighbor. I mean their estates are separated by some fifty acres or so but . . . Christ, this is too bizarre."

been unpacked that morning from a trunk that hadn't been opened in a decade, but then few police officers received sartorial awards. Norton wondered if there was a Mrs. Sparks and an assortment of offspring.

"Do us both a favor. Go easy." Sparks was lighting a fresh cheroot.

"On who?"

"I'm talking about you. I have a feeling you're smarter than your late friend was, but still . . . go easy. I'd hate to see you end up the same way."

"I plan not to, but then, the best laid plans . . . and all that jazz." Norton got to his feet. "I'll go for a drive now and do some thinking."

Sparks arose and held out his hand. Norton shook it. When Norton reached the door and opened it, Sparks said, "Was Clay Stopley really that close a friend of yours?"

"He sure was. I once caught him laying my wife."

Norton didn't wait for the detective's reaction and shut the door behind him. What he didn't see was the cheroot drop from Sparks's mouth onto the desk.

Half an hour later, Norton was steering the rented Renault along a secluded road in Coldwater Canyon. He had a reasonable idea as to the location of Hagar Simon's castle and wanted a look at it. It was on every tourist's itinerary and pinpointed on every map of the stars' homes sold throughout Los Angeles. While some maps were out of date and many stars had since moved on to other quarters or foreign locations, the houses remained, to satisfy the appetites of the insatiably curious. The car tooled along slowly, while Norton tried to erase from his mind the ugly sight of Clay Stopley's battered body. Pushed or fallen from a rampart? Crushed by a gorilla? Or theory X, the unknown, the surprise answer. His last contact with Clay had been six days before his death. It was the afternoon of the day of his first (perhaps his only?) invitation from Hagar Simon.

"I've been sweating it out for a week," said Clay over the telephone, "and I finally got the phone call this morning. It

"He intimates Hagar Simon is clean as a whistle."

"From where he sits, why not? He doesn't know what we know."

"And what do *we* know?"

"I hope we'll know more after tonight. Don't overplay it. Just ingratiate yourself with your hostess, and get what you can on the other guests. Don't go prowling around on your own. You taking Frost?"

"She's taking me. The invitation came through her."

"Interesting."

"She's gorgeous. What do I do if there's some sort of circus tonight?"

"Need I tell you?"

Clay emitted a lewd chuckle. "These are the kinds of jobs I *really* like."

"Clay, be very careful. This assignment's no lark. You're up against a very tough, very dangerous syndicate."

"You don't have to remind me," said Clay soberly. "I'm just humming to give myself courage. You intending to make contact with Lila Frank in New York?"

"Not unless it's accidentally. She's covered herself with three bookings out of New York back to L.A. next week. I'm booked on all three. Whichever she takes, I'll be on it, sitting right next to her."

"Careful. I'm told she bites."

"Keep in touch."

Keep in touch, but Clay never called again. That wasn't unusual. If there had been anything important, he would have heard. Or perhaps the idiot had decided to play the lone wolf until he discovered something spectacular. Well, he certainly discovered something. If he hadn't, he'd be alive today, enjoying the view with Norton. And the view was spectacular. Before him through a windshield loomed Hagar's castle, a formidable sight. He'd seen nothing like it since a boat trip up the Rhine shortly after his divorce from Marti. (Why the hell can't I rid myself of the memory of you, you stinking nymphomaniac!) Norton concentrated on the

The son of a bitch is probably still trying to decide between Al Smith and Herbert Hoover. Udo Yosaka. Japanese financial wizard. What do those factories of his process besides frozen foods? Hash? Heroin? Scopolamine? What? Viola Pickfair and Chloe Jupiter.

That's *got* to be Chloe's estate!

Norton was glancing out the right window at a lavish, pink, heart-shaped mansion. Heart-shaped! Leave it to Chloe Jupiter. Showmanship begins at home. He would have to meet Chloe. He could do that through her niece. She's Hagar's neighbor. She dines at the castle. She's a shrewd old owl. Nothing would escape her. Irving, the gorilla. Damn it. Could Chloe Jupiter be part of Hagar's action? He hoped not. She'd been his pinup girl at elementary school. He had her seductive portrait taped to the inside of the door of his gymnasium locker. Chloe Jupiter in *Belle Of The Brawl*. He'd seen that one six times.

There must have been others at Hagar Simon's that Monday night. There had to be. And Clay Stopley had to have been there too. It made sense. He could feel it. He steered the car toward Sunset Boulevard.

He hoped Karen Frost was listed in the telephone directory.

very soon he would have to put his second cover story into operation. Norton Valentine as stockbroker would suffice for the moment, but eventually he would have to become the private investigator hired by Clay's family to investigate his horrible death. Clay's family had already been briefed, in case anyone tried to double-check.

Viola Pickfair? No. Scrub it. Let it wait until tomorrow. Don't push it. Go slow, he cautioned himself, go easy. Don't go out of your way to invite any sudden brushes with death like the one in Dallas after the Kennedy assassination.

He thought about Chloe Jupiter and smiled. He could still liberally quote dialogue from all of her films. He saw her on the witness stand in *The Men In My Wife,* irritated by a cross-examining defense attorney in the breach of promise suit reminding her of a former lover. "What wuz that name y'mentioned? Don Pedro San Alvarez? Hmmmmm . . ." Chloe examined the courtroom ceiling and then the all male jury as she seductively crossed a leg and stroked her long sable stole. She turned to the defense attorney, bristling with indignation, "Why shuah, I remember that there Don Pedro San Alvarez. Why he wuz'n' good enough tuh put in muh diary."

The telephone rang. Norton sat up. He let the phone ring two more times and then answered, "Hello?"

"Norton Valentine?" Very cool and sexy. He murmured acknowledgment. "This is Karen Frost. It's not true about Clay, is it?" She sounded genuinely concerned. Genuinely concerned or like an actress who deserved a better break than she'd been getting.

"Yes, it is, I'm sorry to say."

"But how awful." There was a slight choke in her voice, and Norton wanted to believe it was unrehearsed. "How did it happen? Was it a heart attack?"

"I'd rather tell you in person, if it's possible. I know Clay thought a great deal of you. He phoned me in New York about a week ago on some business."

"Did he? I don't think he ever mentioned you."

was badly in need of recovering. For five years she had pleaded with him to redecorate and refurnish his home, but it was easier to get Hartley to part with a confidence than with cash.

"I didn't talk to Harvey Tripp. I talked to Phyllis Grain, his secretary."

"Where's Tripp?" she asked sharply.

"Off in parts unknown. What difference does it make? Miss Grain is attached at his hip. She's been with him since Moses parted the Red Sea. She okayed Valentine."

"How okay?" She glanced impatiently at her wristwatch.

He leaned forward slightly and inquired woozily, "Did you say you had a date?"

"Yes, I said I had a date, Burton. I'm meeting Czardi at the Greek Theater in half an hour."

"Oh? What's on there?"

"Four Fokine ballets. Now, come on, let's get back to Valentine." She hated herself for being impatient with him, but she knew his continued lucidity was now a matter of minutes.

"Oh, yes, Norton Valentine." He stared into his drink, as though Norton's credentials were being teleflashed there. "He's with Brixton and Sons, and you know where they stand on Wall Street."

"Go on."

"He goes by the title of Securities Analyst, which means he does a lot of dirty work. Hatchet man. He can manipulate a stock to look good, or he can send it plummeting. If he's for you, you get rich; if he's against you, you get headlines. The S.E.C. can't get a thing on him."

"He sounds like a presidential candidate."

"Miss Grain has no information, of course, as to his mission in Los Angeles, except be nice to him and try and find out what he's up to, because whatever it is could certainly be of use. Shall I pass this on to Hagar?"

"You'll pass out before you can pass on."

"Don't be cruel. Please don't be cruel."

prostitutes of the Fourth Estate who would leap at the chance to replace me and obey instructions faithfully."

Lila leapt to her feet with her eyes aimed at his face and her mouth open to fire. "I broke my back to get the old man to hold on to you, and you're staying!"

"Don't shout. You're making my ice cubes melt."

"There's no replacing you now, and you damned well know it. There's nobody else we know of we can trust, and there's no time to look for him. That was the argument I used, and by God, you're going to back me up or . . ."

". . . Or?"

Her anger abated, and a twinkle came to her eyes. She placed her hands on his shoulders and lightly kissed his cheek. "Or I'll hire you a trained nurse, and make you go cold turkey."

"Fat chance," he said with a snort. She moved away from him and gathered up her evening bag and gloves. "Who'd you say you were meeting?"

She sighed and told him, "Mickey Czardi."

"Ah yes. Count Miklos Czardi. I do hope his company is more palatable than the dreadful cuisine he serves in his restaurant."

"He only sells it. He doesn't eat it."

"I remember him when he was a man without friends or credit cards."

"Hungarians don't need friends, and they print their own credit cards."

"Won't his glamorous girl friend be with him tonight?"

"No, darling. You know how it is in this town. Two's company; three's a coproduction." She headed for the door.

"I love you, Lila."

She opened the door and said over her shoulder, "Likewise, darling. Talk to you in the morning."

Hartley didn't hear the door shut. He sat staring with glazed eyes at the palm of his limp right hand, as though hoping to read among the lines some sign of a brighter future.

"Now isn't that funny? I was just thinking of having one myself." She reached for a bottle of tequila and a pitcher and began mixing the drinks. "Be a doll, and do the salt on the glasses."

"Where's the salt?"

"Right here." She reached under the counter and produced an apothecary jar filled with salt. Norton spread salt on a dish and deftly coated the rims of the glasses with a professional twist of the wrist, while wondering if her dark glasses were an affectation or a curtain behind which were hidden unmentionable secrets. The expression on her face as she lazily stirred the contents of a pitcher belonged on Mount Rushmore. Karen broke the conversational deadlock. "Tell me about Clay." He told her what he knew without sparing the more gruesome details. As he spoke, her hand began to shake, and then she released her hold on the stirrer and clamped her hand over her mouth, turning away from him.

"I'm sorry. I should have edited some of the details." He watched her lift the glass and dab at her eyes with a cocktail napkin. "When did you last see him?" He was working hard at keeping his tone casual.

"Last Thursday night, I guess it was. I left for Palm Springs the next morning. I posed for a fashion layout there." Composure regained, she poured the drinks and led the way to a sofa.

"Did he happen to mention an invitation to Hagar Simon's for Monday night?"

She hesitated for a moment and then said, "Not that I remember." Norton knew she wished she sounded convincing. "As far as I know, he's only been to Hagar's once, and that was as my escort."

"How'd you meet Clay?"

"A mutual friend of ours in New York told him to look me up. He caught me on a very lonely night, and so I accepted his invitation to dinner."

"I can't imagine you having many lonely nights."

"You'd be surprised." She faced him with a winsome

— 33 —

"Is that what the police think?"

"They interrogated Mrs. Simon and four of her guests. All of them insist Clay wasn't there."

Her body relaxed. "Well then . . ."

"I think it's a conspiracy of silence. There were probably other guests besides these four. I suppose Ira Sparks—he's the detective handling the case—didn't press for the rest of the guest list because he figured he'd get the same discouraging results."

"Oh dear, why do so many people find the truth discouraging?"

"Why would so many people agree to a lie?"

"Mr. Valentine . . ."

"Please call me Norton, Miss Frost."

"All right, Norton," she said melodiously, "why would so many people conspire to a lie?"

"Because murder can have such disagreeable consequences. 'Scandal' is an unpleasant word in everybody's vocabulary. Hagar Simon's guest lists are a homogeneous variety of the famous and the infamous."

She drained her glass and then said, "You know so much about Hagar. Is private investigating one of your hobbies?"

"No, but I get around. I meet a lot of people. I've met people who've been to Mrs. Simon's parties. I've had an earful. Do you like the woman?"

"There are things about her I admire."

"Such as what? Her wealth? Her position? Her parties?"

"Mostly her needlepoint," she replied sarcastically.

Norton smiled. "You're a real cool chick." With a lightning movement, he removed her dark glasses.

"*Hey!*" she yelped and jumped to her feet, the glass slipping from her hand and shattering on the floor. There was an ugly bruise around her right eye.

"Don't step on any glass," he cautioned her.

"That wasn't very nice, *Norton.*"

"Neither's your eye. That birdie looks about two or three days old."

behind him and then got to his feet, hands raised with open palms in defeat. "Okay, okay! I'm going! Reluctantly, but I'm going." She had hurried to the door and now pulled it open with a violent jerk. Norton strolled casually to the exit.

"Sorry about that smartass crack."

"Get out of here!" Her left hand connected with his back with surprising strength, and he stumbled into the hall, the door slamming shut behind him.

"Norton," he said to the ceiling, "that was very poorly handled."

"I don't see any Norton," said a concertina voice behind him. He turned and looked into the face of a snub-nosed, raven-haired pixie wearing slacks and a see-through blouse.

"*I* am Norton," he said, with his arms folded.

"You shouldn't go around talking to yourself because people who talk to themselves are the cruel victims of a loneliness syndrome and that could lead to serious injury to the psyche and the id and a one-way ticket to cuckoo land . . ."

"Oh, God, spare me," he gasped and rushed past her. Had he been in less of a hurry, he would have seen her press the bell to Karen Frost's apartment and then babble to a furious Karen when she opened the door, "So who was the john named Norton who talks to himself outside your door wearing those obscene blue jeans with thighs that look hard enough to crack coconuts and Jesus you're breaking my wrist . . ."

Karen pulled her inside and slammed the door hard.

Norton pulled away from the curb and headed toward Sunset Boulevard. There were no people strolling on North Kings Road, and the only sign of activity was the white Thunderbird behind him, which he saw in a glance at his rearview mirror. He shifted his thoughts to Karen Frost. That early surface innocence had brilliantly masked a poisonous flower. That hard shove out the door. That's big strength for a little lady. The sudden eruption of violent staring out the window at the swimming pool. He wished there was somebody out there he could talk to. He hadn't felt this lonely since the day his divorce decree became final.

Count Miklos Czardi was looking across the table with displeasure at Lila Frank. They were seated in a circular booth of his restaurant facing the crowded bar. His frown intensified as she continued to ignore him, her eyes scanning the room for celebrities, while his anger gave a saturnine cast to his fading Magyar looks.

"Isn't it enough you dragged me out of the theatre in the middle of the Black Swan pas de deux without compounding the felony by ignoring me in my *own* restaurant?"

"I've seen better dancing by paraplegics," she said offhandedly, while drumming the table top with her fingers.

"Would you like another drink?" he asked with irritation.

"I haven't started this one."

"Shall we order dinner?"

"After I finish the drink."

"You're behaving objectionably."

She stared at him with hooded eyes. "Stop pushing me."

"I don't like being ignored. What's the matter with you tonight?"

She placed an elbow on the table and cupped her chin with the hand. "Heavy heavy hangs over my head. Ever experience the feeling?"

"Many times," he countered with an imperious sniff. "When my father lost his vast estates in Transylvania, and we had to flee the Nazis in an oxcart . . ."

"Oh, save that crap for Radie Harris."

"You never believe anything I tell you." He allowed himself a dramatic pause and then spoke with a tear in his voice. "Poor Daddy . . . killed by a bayonet thrust through the straw at the border . . ."

"Your father died of an abcessed fang."

"You're close," he said warmly. "Actually, it was a gangrene infection from an injury suffered from a disgusting habit

— 39 —

gesture of straightening his bow tie. "I'm a highly honored and respected citizen of my adopted country . . ."

"Oh, shut up, and get me another drink. This one tastes like piss." A waiter responded to Czardi's signal in a flash.

"I think we should also order some food," insisted Czardi.

Lila snapped at the waiter, "Bring me a club sandwich, and leave out the club." Czardi ordered a minute steak, and the waiter left. Lila lit a cigarette and resumed her celebrity spotting, while Czardi beamed at the crush at the bar.

"Business is magnificent tonight. I wish I could keep every nickel of it."

"You keep enough," drawled Lila, "Heifetz would envy the way you fiddle your books."

Czardi ignored the insult and espied a celebrated film star standing near the cashier's desk. "That woman with Roy Hunter looks like his father."

"Where's Roy Hunter?"

"They're near the cashier's desk."

Lila leaned forward and squinted. "That *is* his father." And then her range of vision encompassed a familiar figure perched on a stool at the far corner of the bar. "Well, well, well," she muttered.

"Well, well, well, *what?*"

"Norton Valentine's at the bar."

Czardi levitated and craned his neck. "Which one? The white turtleneck in the far corner?" Lila nodded. "I wonder why the dumb grin on his face."

"Looks like he's trying to make it with the brunette gargoyle wearing the hot pants."

"Oh, yes. She's one of our regulars."

"She looks so dear," said Lila with a tinge of venom.

"She's very dear," Czardi confirmed, "but she'll come down in price."

Norton wasn't in the least bit interested in the brunette. He was studying two men at the opposite end of the bar who had followed him into the restaurant. Their white Thunderbird was several spaces away from his car in the parking lot mustered an expression of shock on her face that could have done with additional rehearsal. "I had to go to the morgue to confirm the identification. It was a brutal sight. His name was Clay Stopley."

"Clay Stopley . . . Clay Stopley . . ." Lila repeated the name, as though she hoped to build up an immunity to it. "Mickey? Didn't we meet a Clay Stopley at Hagar's a couple of weeks ago?"

Czardi intertwined his fingers and clenched them tightly. "Yes, as a matter of fact, I think we might have."

"He was with a girl named Karen Frost," said Norton helpfully.

"Of course!" Lila shook her head sadly. "Now I remember him. Such a good-looking guy, too."

"He's lost those looks," said Norton and, with subtle sadistic relish, described the corpse as he had seen it at the morgue.

"Oh, my God," gasped Lila, while clutching at her throat, "cancel my sandwich. How terrible for you, Norton. How really terrible. Now, I remember. He was in Wall Street too. I remember overhearing him advising someone to dump their Columbia Pictures stock. Dave Begelman, as I recall." She placed a damp palm over Norton's hand. "You poor guy. I hope this doesn't upset the deal you're working on."

Norton patted her hand gently while the waiter served the fresh drinks. "No, but it does complicate matters a bit. Most of the information I needed was in poor Clay's battered head."

Lila withdrew her hand and gazed at Czardi. "Mickey, darling, you're perspiring. Why don't you have them turn up the air conditioning?"

Czardi dabbed at his forehead with a napkin. "I wonder if Karen knows."

"She does," said Norton. "I had a drink with her at her place."

"Oh did you?" Lila toyed with her pearls. "Was she very upset when you told her?"

"Yes. She dropped a glass."

"Funny, Lila, I'm only getting a lot of hot air."

"Norton, I think there's more to you than meets the eye." She leaned toward him cozily. "Come on, be good to a news hen. What's the *real* story? I haven't had a decent scoop since I bought some ice cream a couple of weeks ago. I know Ira Sparks. He's a-okay in my books. If you don't level with me, he will."

"So help me, all I know is what I've told you," insisted Norton, hoping it sounded sincere. "The only thing I've left out is the possibility he might have been at Hagar Simon's the night he was killed." He wasn't sure if Czardi had squelched a belch or was still fighting for air. Lila's eyebrows were rising slowly, and Norton wondered if they would join her hairline.

"What does Hagar say?"

"She says no." Norton told her about Hagar and the four guests.

"Well, if they say he wasn't there, then, darling Norton, he certainly wasn't there." One of her hands was out of sight under the table, and Norton wondered if her fingers were crossed. "How'd you know about Karen Frost?" Norton repeated an abridged version of his phone conversation with Clay Stopley the previous week. Lila's hand surfaced and patted Norton's cheek. "You leave the investigating to the professionals. Ira doesn't look like much, but he delivers. And as to those two bums trailing you, just tell Ira. If they are, he'll get them off your back."

"Oh, I don't mind them," said Norton with his stupid grin. "I think they're kind of fun. I wonder if either of them plays Scrabble."

Lila grinned. "Norton, you're real cute. I'm glad we ran into each other tonight." She turned to Czardi. "Wasn't I lucky sitting next to him on the jet?" She smiled at Norton. "Now you don't have to phone me tomorrow morning. We can make a date for dinner right now."

"Well, if we do, it'll have to be a tentative one."

"Why?"

4

Slowly, Norton got to his feet, terrified that at any moment they might buckle. His temples throbbed, and his mouth felt paralyzed. He'd often wondered how he would react should this moment arrive, and now the moment was here, and his behavior was nothing like the mental image he had prepared for himself. He was neither suave nor blasé and couldn't think of a quip with which to put them both at ease. He held his hand out stiffly, and she brushed it lightly with her fingertips, a polite smile on her face, her eyes gently mocking.

"How nice to meet you," purred the enchanting tigress as she squeezed in next to Czardi. "I didn't hear your last name."

"Valentine," he said swiftly and sat down. *I didn't hear your last name*. I thank you for that, sweetheart. I thank you for not giving the game away. I thank you for waiting until I get a chance to explain, if I get the chance to explain.

And then he thought of something that made his blood run cold. She knows these two extremely well. She would know Hagar Simon. She might have been at the castle Monday

Brixton and Sons, which we were supposed to settle together. I'll have to retrace what he'd accomplished."

"How tiresome for you."

"But necessary."

The waiter arrived with Lila and Czardi's food. "What took you so long?" snapped Lila. "Did you have to go over to Chasen's to get it?" She lifted a gherkin and circumsized it with a ferocious bite.

"Are you hungry, Marti, darling?" asked Czardi, staring at his minute steak as though it had offended him.

"No, thank you. I had some scrambled eggs at home. How was the ballet?"

"As bad as this rotten sandwich," growled Lila through a mouthful of food. "The bacon's soggy, the chicken is tough, the tomatoes are tasteless, and, thank God, it's on the house." Norton thought of putting it on her head. Lila saw him staring at her food. "You want the rest of this? If you don't, I'm sending it over to the Board of Health."

"As a matter of fact, I'm famished." He moved the plate in front of him and dug in with relish, while Lila glowered at Czardi who chewed on a piece of steak with mincing movements of his mouth.

"Marti." Marti turned to Lila. "Is Karen very upset about Stopley?"

"Very."

"How's her black eye?" They stared at Norton. "That's quite a mouse she's got. She told me she fell off a horse in Palm Springs."

"Yes, she did," said Marti. "Karen'll never learn to sit a horse well. She'll never learn when to give them their head."

"Must have been tough on your photographer, posing her to keep that left eye hidden."

"He managed rather artistically, as a matter of fact."

And so are you, Marti, sweetheart, still lying as artistically as always. It's her right eye that took the punishment. You girls should have taken more time getting your stories

— 49 —

leave the driving to us. Now, Marti, *dar*ling, what the hell's this crap with Palm Springs and Karen's black eye?"

Norton made it back to the hotel without the Thunderbird escort. He undressed quickly, put on a robe, and mixed himself a nightcap. He turned out the living room lights and sat by the window staring out at the swimming pool. He welcomed Marti to his thoughts with open qualms. He wasn't kidding himself about still being in love with her. He was. It disgusted him to know she was sharing Czardi's bed. It frightened him that she was mixed up in the Hagar scene. She'd know soon enough how unsuccessful was her attempt to shore up Karen Frost's Palm Springs alibi. Karen must have been at Hagar's with Clay on Monday night. Marti could have been there too, with Czardi.

Marti couldn't have betrayed Clay. If she had, then she would have blown his own cover at the restaurant. Of course. She's protecting herself. She's in deep with this gang. How could she admit her ex-husband is a secret service man? Innocence be damned with vultures like these; they'd condemn her as guilty by past association. On the other hand, if she had fingered Clay, she could be spilling the beans about him right now.

Oh, Christ.

He began pacing the room. Did she or didn't she? Would she or wouldn't she? There was nothing in the manual to cover a situation like this. He sighed and sat down again. He'd have to play it by ear. Meet whatever emergency whenever it arose. But not like Clay. He would not let himself get cornered, beaten up and flung to his death. Marti heard him say Doheny Dauphin. She'll call. She'll be in touch somehow. Maybe she isn't fully aware of what she's gotten herself into. Czardi's probably just a way station for her, until someone better comes along. How the hell could she let that sweating pig touch her? *Count* Miklos Czardi. He reached for the phone, dialed, made a quick connection,

I handle it my way." He listened again. "I'm sure I'll hear from Marti. The minute she thinks it's safe, I know I'll hear from her. By the way, there's a tail on me." He described the two men and their car. "They're very obvious, and it could be deliberate. They don't know I don't frighten easy." He listened and laughed and then hung up.

He stared at the phone he'd been talking into, loathing its turquoise color. Turquoise was Marti's favorite. The phone was a private one, not connected with the switchboard, installed before his arrival by prior arrangement. It was nothing unusual for the Doheny Dauphin. Most transients who did most of their work by telephone preferred a private instrument for outgoing calls. It was less expensive, and the hotel preferred it because it was less of a burden on the switchboard. Only the hotel, the telephone company and Norton's associates across the country knew of its existence and the private number.

While opting for a second nightcap, he wondered who had blackened Karen Frost's eye and why. Was it her dubious reward for the attempted bravery at defying an order? Maybe she'd really been hung up on Clay, knew the identity of his killer, demanded justice regardless of the consequences to herself. It would be nice to believe that, thought Norton. He had sampled some of her spirit and, in retrospect, admired it. Would he sample it again once she realized how tough a spot she was in? He hoped so. He needed her information. He needed information from all of them, either directly or by a slip of the tongue.

Hagar Simon's castle was a clearinghouse for evil. There had been and probably were setups similar to hers in London, Paris, Rome and God knows where else, possibly even in some remote outbacks missionaries hadn't heard of. Powerful men and distinguished careers were being deliberately and systematically broken to benefit one perfidious organization with a lust and greed for power unequaled since the pillaging and rampaging of the early Roman conquerors. And you couldn't pin a thing on Hagar. You couldn't cog in the machinery, an innocent lamb among wolves. Even knowing her for what she had been and undoubtedly still was, he was still in love with her. It was seeing her that evening and feeling the old pang of jealousy that confirmed his feelings. So be it.

After four hours of troubled sleep, Norton awoke shortly before eight, shaved, showered, ordered breakfast and a newspaper. There was a three paragraph item about Clay on the lower, left-hand column on the third page. Murdered man found in Griffith Park. Nothing exotic enough about the killing to rate a headline. No severed head, no celebrity, just a solitary victim of murder, small pickings for this genocidal generation. Norton checked his horoscope, making a mental promise to himself to obey its injunctions to tidy up his house and find out why a friend was feeling ignored and then flung the papers on the couch. He hoped Viola Pickfair was an early riser. If she wasn't, she was about to be rudely awakened. He consulted his address book and dialed.

Viola Pickfair sounded as though she'd been up for hours wakening roosters. The voice was perky with bubbles and fizz and even adolescently petulant, as Norton heard, "I hope this is the exterminator because I can still hear that poor little mouse squealing in my woodwork and don't tell me I've got bats in my belfry because how can a little mouse survive in my woodwork after three days and if it got in there why isn't it smart enough to find its way out and oh my God there it goes again so what kind of an exterminator are you when I phoned you on Tuesday and here it is Thursday and I have to have my hair done . . ."

"Miss Pickfair!" Norton shouted.

"Speaking."

"This is *not* the exterminator."

"Then why are you calling?"

"My name is Norton Valentine. I . . ."

"*Norton.* You mean Norton who was standing in the hallway outside Karen's door last night talking to the ceiling 'Norton that was very poorly handled' or something like that

— 55 —

Thirty minutes later, carrying the bag of groceries, Norton stood on Viola Pickfair's threshhold. She lived in a ramshackle cottage on San Vincente just a few streets from his hotel. Viola held the door open staring at him with open disappointment.

"Awwwww you're not wearing your blue jeans." She wriggled to one side. "Come on in anyway because I like your open shirt it looks so sexy with that hair on your chest and here give me that bag and let's go into the kitchen because it's the cleanest and my purse is there and how much did all this cost and I hope you remembered to collect the green stamps because I'm saving up for a relaxercycle because Aunt Chloe says my bust needs developing . . ."

Norton swam with the stream of monologue into the kitchen, where she deposited the milk in the refrigerator and the other groceries on the shelf and then found her purse and meticulously counted out the coins with which to repay him. Counterpointing the business and the continuous flow of stream of consciousness, Norton studied the girl and decided that in repose, if ever, she would be an uncommonly beautiful little creature. She was barely five feet tall, and now with her hair in pigtails, wearing a man's shirt and pedal pushers, she resembled a backwoods gamin.

"I'll bet you think I'm cute," she said as though reading his mind.

"Very cute."

"Weeellll I'm older than you think but I won't tell you how much and I just made a fresh pot of coffee so let's have some okay?"

Once the coffee was poured and they sat around the small circular kitchen table, Viola appeared to have run out of steam and sat like a small child on her first day at school, waiting for Norton to make the next move. He took a sip of coffee, savored it, and said, "You make very good coffee."

"Thank you," she said, with a small voice, "and I'm really sorry about what happened to Clay. Karen told me you were good friends so I know how you must be feeling."

"Oh yeah . . . she introduces me to all the producers and directors and casting agents she knows because she doesn't feel any rivalry the way other women do and she knows and so does everybody else know I don't want to get ahead on my Aunt Chloe's reputation which is why I changed my name from Selma O'Flaherty to Viola Pickfair . . . Viola is my favorite instrument and Pickfair is where Mary Pickford lives with Buddy Rogers her husband who supplanted in her affections the late Douglas Fairbanks Senior who first lived at Pickfair with Mary . . ."

"Who socked Karen in the eye?"

"She fell off a horse."

"In Palm Springs."

"That's right . . . Palm Springs."

"She was there on a job with Marti Leigh."

"She was?" Norton smiled gently. "That's right! She was there with Marti Leigh!"

"Viola."

"Yes?" she said meekly.

"I think it's all a trumped up story." Viola appeared to be on the verge of tears. "I think Karen knows more about Clay's murder than she dares to tell, and somebody socked her in the eye as a warning."

There was a catch in Viola's voice, as she insisted, "Honest Karen's a wonderful girl . . . she adored Clay she really did. She's all broken up about it . . . I mean after you left her she just cried and cried and gee it made her eye look even worse."

"Were you there when she phoned Marti Leigh?"

"No," came the swift response, "she phoned her after I left."

"How do you know?"

"How do I know?"

"How do you know?"

"Because . . ." she stared at the stove for a moment before continuing ". . . because I called her before I went to bed to see if she was feeling better and she said she was feeling

"She was my favorite movie star. I used to have her picture taped to the inside of my gymnasium locker when I was a kid at school."

"If she'll see you don't tell her how many years ago that was."

"Would you call her?"

Viola thought for a moment, then sighed, and said, "Okay." She turned off the water tap and disappeared into the living room. Norton left his chair and stared out a window into Viola's backyard. There was a child's swing, a sandbox and an overgrowth of weeds. Viola the child-woman forced to play adult games. Tossed by chance into a cesspool situation. Instructed to lie but not even good enough an actress to carry that off. Maybe Monday was her first night at Hagar Simon's. Maybe she really hadn't seen Clay there. Maybe I'm kidding myself and she's actually a better actress than all of them. But there were too many slips. Too many delicious slips. The madras jacket. The black eye. Palm Springs. Marti.

"Aunt Chloe says you can come over in an hour."

He hadn't heard her return and then realized why. She had removed her shoes. "Thanks a lot, Viola. I appreciate this." Then, like a whirlwind, she rushed across the room and threw her arms around him, pressing her cheek tightly against his bared chest.

"It's only fifteen minutes from here to Aunt Chloe's which gives us plenty of time for a quick one what do you say Norton I really dig you the most!"

Some child-woman.

Very gently, he pried her loose from him and cupped her face in his hands and looked into her hungry little eyes. He bent his head and kissed her hotly while his tongue pried her mouth open and counted her teeth. Then he whispered gently, "I'll try to send the rest over later."

"You fink!" she snarled, and went stomping to the front door, pulling it open for him. "You won't get anything out of Aunt Chloe either! She just wants to see what you look like!"

"Thanks for the coffee and the kiss." She stared at him

5

Norton spent an exhilarating hour leading the white Thunderbird on a tour of Hollywood. He had started the morning with a full tank and hoped they hadn't. He flirted with traffic violations by jumping lights and making turns from the wrong lanes, but the boys on his tail kept right with him. He was tempted to pick up a hitchhiker on Wilshire Boulevard, but from the leer on the boy's face, he could guess his desired destination was the nearest bedroom for a modest fee. At precisely one hour from the time he left Viola Pickfair's cottage, Norton passed Hagar Simon's castle and pulled into Chloe Jupiter's driveway. He saw the Thunderbird slow down and settle across the road from Chloe's under a shade tree. In the glare of a blazing sun, the heart-shaped house resembled an expensive French dessert. Norton took the steps leading to the front door two at a time, pressed the bell, and heard the chimes tinkling the opening bars of "Bewitched, Bothered and Bewildered."

After what seemed like an interminable wait, Norton was about to press the bell again when the door slowly opened. Norton was staggered by the sight confronting him. He saw ders for the past two hours." He looked at Norton with an impish grin. "Miss Jupiter never suffers an energy crisis."

"Don't brag, Horace," Norton heard from behind him. "Just mix the drink." Norton turned and saw the fabulous lady entering through a panel in the wall that slid shut behind her. She advanced slowly, hands delicately placed on her hips, blazing red hair crowned by a glittering tiara, a diaphanous gown carefully tailored to accentuate every curve of her amazingly youthful-looking body, the hips undulating as he had seen them undulate in dozens of films. Her skin was unlined ivory, and though the eyes were heavily made up, there was but a trace of orange lipstick. She wasn't much taller than her niece, yet gave the impression of a statuesque beauty. Though she looked years younger, Norton knew she was old enough to be his mother and was glad she wasn't. She stopped a few feet away from him and slowly surveyed him from head to toe, like an art expert examining a potential purchase.

"Ummmm, uh, Norton, . . . uh hope the neighbors saw yuh comin' up the driveway. . . . It might change muh image around here." Norton couldn't find his voice but managed his stupid grin. Her eyes studied his face again and then slowly traveled downward. "Ummmmmuh, Norton, . . . uh see you're not unarmed." He blushed while she smiled the famous smile that bespoke a private joke. "Yuh look nervous, Norton. Would you like a tranquilizer, honey?"

He found his voice. "I guess I'm a bit overwhelmed, Miss Jupiter."

"Why, of course yuh are, Norton. Uh sympathize. Sit over there in the easy chair, Norton, and take it easy. Uh'll sit over here right across from yuh an' continue feastin'. Hurry up with them drinks, Horace."

"Coming right up."

"Uh hope yuh mean the drinks." She smiled at Norton, who was trying to look comfortable and at ease. "Viola tells me yuh one of muh fans. Is this a business call or a pilgrimage?"

glass back on the table. "Uh drove most of 'em there. A woman what lives by the Bible, Norton, don't like lyin'. But yuh see, Norton, like a lotta works of art, uh'm a flawed masterpiece. Uh know what yuh're after. It's this Clay Stopley business. Uh read the piece on him in the *Times* this mornin'. Not much of a piece, was it? He should fire his press agent." She slowly wriggled to her feet and paced the floor. Norton now realized she was wearing platform shoes. "Uh mean uh already said muh piece to that detective man, Sparks." She stopped in front of Norton and stared down at him. "Uh like yuh looks better. Yuh're Ivy League, uh can tell. Uh gotta green thumb. Uh suppose yuh wonderin' if uh'm tryin' tuh protect Hagar just because we're neighbors. Well, uh ain't." She resumed her slow, measured pacing. "Uh don't much like Hagar, and uh told Isaac he was a fool tuh marry her. Why, when he first introduced me tuh her, she was so dumb, she was confused by indoor plumbin'. Of course, she's learned a lot since then. But, yuh see, she still lives in the past. She's still readin' *Anthony Adverse*.

"Uh don't make no bones about muh age. Uh'm proud of it and the fact uh don't look it. That's because uh live for today. Uh move along with the times. That's why, every generation, uh win a million new fans. The kids today worship me the way their fathers and, yeah, their grandfathers did. Uh mean there's one old beau of mine uh visit every week in the veteran's hospital what still remembers my theatrical dayboo in *The Mikado*."

"Really?" said Norton. "What part did you play?"

"Well, whaddya think?" she said, sauntering toward him slowly then stopping a few inches from his face and gently grinding her hips. "Yum Yum."

The effect was too much for Norton. He burst into laughter, and after a beat, she joined in with him.

"Norton, uh really think uh like yuh. Yuh can tell when uh'm puttin' yuh on. Yuh know, muh career's the biggest put-on in show business history. Of course, uh'm enjoyin' the joke more than anybody else. Uh mean, uh'm glad yuh know back to her chair and sat while Norton stood transfixed with eyes glued to the opening in the wall.

The gorilla entered slowly, wet eyes blinking. Irving and Norton examined each other with equal interest. "Come over here, Irvin'," commanded Chloe, "and crouch at muh feet. Come on over here, Norton, and shake hands with Irvin'." As the gorilla settled in position at Chloe's feet, Norton slowly moved forward. "Well, come on, Norton," said Chloe impatiently, "he ain't gonna hurt yuh. Irvin' is a lamb. Uh've had him since he was a pup. He's been tutored by some of the best teachers money can buy. He's got a higher I.Q. than any William Morris agent. D'yuh know Princeton College is beggin' for his brain when he dies? Uh won't give 'em no commitment unless they offer him first a honorary degree. Now don't be coy, Irvin', and shake Norton's hand. He's muh friend. He's got class, can'tcha tell?"

Gently, the gorilla took Norton's hand in his own and shook it.

"Now how about *that!*" exclaimed Chloe triumphantly to Norton. "Was that the grip of a killer? Besides, he's got a alibi for Monday night. He was here with Horace X. and Horace's mother Louella—she's muh puhsonal maid—watchin' television. Irvin' never misses 'M.A.S.H.'" Irving's eyes brightened. "Uh don't understand it m'self, but he's nuts about Alan Alda. Go ahead, Norton, if yuh wanna question Irvin'. Well, don't look so dumb. He understands English. Uh told yuh he was smart. Why, when some of muh friends come over for a friendly game of charades, everybody fights tuh get Irvin' on their team."

Norton could feel the perspiration trickling down his back. It was too bizarre, too weird, too unreal for him. He actually believed he saw a smug expression on Irving as the gorilla blithely examined a fingernail. "I . . . er . . . don't doubt that he has an alibi."

"Why, of course, he has an alibi. Uh told yuh before, uh live by the good book. All right Irvin', yuh can go back tuh

"Norton Valentine's my real name."

"Well, yuh'll have tuh change it for movin' pitchers."

"And I know I can trust you."

"Yuh better believe it," she said warmly.

"I'm a government investigator. A secret service man."

"Ohhhhh?" Her eyes blazed with renewed interest. "Uh got some secrets yuh could service."

He sat down opposite her. "Clay Stopley was here on a top secret assignment. He slipped up, and he's dead."

She said seriously, "Well, don't yuh go slippin' up."

"I'll do my best not to. Now tell me the truth, *was* Clay at Hagar Simon's Monday night?"

"Ain't yuh afraid muh place is bugged?"

"Is it?"

She smiled slowly. "Yuh know it ain't. Nobody can sneak past my boys."

"What about it. Was Clay there?"

"Yuh muh friend, right?"

"Very right."

"He was there, but yuh didn't hear it from me, right?"

"Chloe Jupiter, I am going to kiss you!"

"Yuh better leave yuh drink on the table, unless yuh like it pipin' hot." He left the drink and his chair and kissed her. "It'll do for now. Now sit down, and yuh listen tuh me, and yuh listen good."

Norton returned to his easy chair and listened. "Uh want yuh tuh understand uh ain't deliberately rattin' on anybody. Yuh see uh'm not all that sure what's really goin' on at Hagar's besides her providin' amusement for a lot of visitin' bigwigs. Now, uh don't like tuh see yuh lookin' so skeptical. Uh know yuh know uh wasn't born yesterday, but uh want yuh to know uh'm like them three Chinese monkeys what don't speak, hear, or see no evil. So just keep yuh face in neutral and listen. Just remember in the old days when uh spoke muh piece, even Clark Gable was all ears. Uh been puttin' two and two t'gether while we been banterin' here.

— 71 —

"Udo Yosaka."

"Yeah, that's him. Not bad lookin' for a Oriental. Now, yuh know uh ain't got no racial prejudices, but while so help me uh'm too young tuh remember the *Maine*, uh sure won't forget Pearl Harbor, so uh couldn't bring muhself tuh be witty and entertain' for the gentleman. Uh also know from past experience the pot was only an appetizer, and while Hagar ain't never been busted, uh ain't one tuh tempt the fates, so uh took muh leave. Uh could use a little of muh mineral water, handsome."

Norton reached for her glass and went to the bar to refill it. He felt lightheaded, and there was a new spring in his step. He was feeling like a slot-machine player hitting the jackpot with his first fifty-cent piece. But, like the player, he was beginning to wonder why it was all so easy, why luck was so suddenly on his side. Was Chloe Jupiter truly on the square, or had she been primed for this interview? There had been an hour between Viola's phone call to her aunt and Norton's arrival for the privileged audience, more than enough time for Chloe to contact the right person or persons and agree on her response. He didn't want to believe that. In any investigation, he was trained to be alert, cautious, and to exercise suspicion, but in Chloe's case, there was one item that caused him to believe she was being genuinely cooperative: the revelation that Karen Frost had been at the castle Monday night. And Norton was convinced that Karen had been intimidated and threatened because she knew or suspected the identity of Clay's killer. He returned to Chloe with the glass of mineral water and realized she had spent the past minute quietly studying him and reading his mind again.

"Yuh wonderin' whether or not tuh trust me," she said, taking the glass from Norton.

"I'm obliged to. It's part of my job."

"Uh got a puhsonal reason for levelin' with yuh, because it has tuh do with muh religious beliefs. It's the commandment that says, 'Thou shalt not kill.' And murder can become a contagious disease. Yuh see uh thought a long time ago

— 73 —

interrupt. Uh'm shuah muh niece was just an innocent bystander that night. Uh mean, uh know she's too dumb to be more than that. Damn it, what uh'm trying' tuh tell yuh is, if yuh can do it, keep her name outta the papers. It's gonna be tough enough tryin' tuh keep muh own out when the time comes." She smiled at Norton. "Uh know when the mud hits the fan, muh name is bound to come up. Uh been tuh so many of her swah-rays. But that was as a favor to a old business associate." She took a deep breath. "Yuh know uh owed muh break in pitchers to Isaac Simon. He took a chance on me when nobody else would. The other studios at the time said uh was too much like muh friend Mae West. Well, neither Mae or me could see the similarity, and for that matter, neither could Isaac. So he put me in that pitcher with his own money. Yuh remember *Queen For A Knight?*"

"I sure do!" acknowledged Norton with gusto.

"Yeah, that was some pitcher. Why when uh sang 'North Pole Papa, Uh Hope You're Goin' South Tonight,' uh not only made screen history, uh got some two hundred theatre managers across the country jailed for impairin' the public morals." She turned to Norton and pointed a finger at him. "It's about then uh turned to religion and started readin' muh Bible. Uh got lotsa favorites in the Old Testament. Like Shadrach, Meshach and ToBedWeGo." She was at Norton's side with a friendly hand on his shoulder. "Now yuh leave Viola tuh me. If she knows anythin' and gives me any trouble about spillin' it, then uh'll get Irvin' tuh squeeze it out of her." Her eyes met Norton's. "Gently, of course. Yuh can believe it when uh tell yuh Irvin' ain't no bone crusher. He's too refeened. Now, Norton, don't take this too puhsonal, but uh'm gonna ask yuh tuh take yuh leave right now." She led the way to the door. "Uh'm a little tired, and uh need muh rest. Now, uh want yuh to write down muh private number and call me anytime yuh feel yuh need tuh talk tuh me, or anythin' else that might come tuh mind." He couldn't see her face, but he imagined she was smiling slyly. She turned slightly and saw he had his address book open with pen and the white Thunderbird. Then her eyes moved slowly to Chloe Jupiter's pastry of a house. Hagar's sigh was colored by a heaviness of heart and a nagging feeling of misgiving and apprehension that worried her nerves like the agonizing pain of a terminal disease.

She found herself of late dwelling on the memory of her respected, albeit unloved, husband Isaac. Isaac had taught her to face the world bravely and with dignity and to ignore the cruel jokes at the expense of her almost nonexistent acting ability. He made her believe in herself as something more than an entertaining novelty who could perform a flawless figure eight and do a breathtaking flying leap through six carefully-spaced burning hoops with a split-second timing that defied the danger of self-immolation. Although now edging fifty, Hagar could still perform an effortless figure eight, still jumped through hoops, and still worried about the hazardous flames.

"Say, what the hell's bothering you?" rasped Lila Frank, studying Hagar from the entrance to the bedroom. Her right hand was choking the neck of a bottle of beer. The other hand held a ham sandwich as though she'd been using it to dust the furniture. She wolfed a bite of sandwich while settling cross-legged on a leather-covered hassock.

"I just saw the boys hot in pursuit of Mr. Valentine. He's been visiting with Chloe." As Hagar spoke, she dropped the fountain pen on a wicker table and placed her hand over the guest list, her tapering lacquered nails resembling organ stops. "Chloe's angry with me. She hasn't forgiven me for urging Viola to remain at the party after Chloe decided to leave. Now Viola's implicated, and Chloe's furious. She came by after lunch yesterday in her coach and four and let me have it in what could hardly be called uncertain terms. She brought the gorilla, and he terrifies the life out of me." She glared at Lila. "I want to go away." Lila continued ruminating thoughtfully. "After tonight's party, I want to go away. I'm not well. You know I'm not well. I need a rest. The doctor on the wicker table and crossed to the guard railing, leaning against it with her arms folded, surveying Hagar with a contempt she usually reserved for a dilatory servant. "You most certainly are not clever, Hagar. What the hell did the old man ever see in you?"

"He couldn't have Chloe. I was second best. And he's got no complaint. I've done my job well. I'm too old for the pill, and I'm too young for social security, and I'm not asking for a pension or a gold watch for faithful service, but I'm owed this much: the right to get away while there's still time."

Lila stared at the sky and entreated, "Mother of Mercy, how do I tell this Snow Queen she's got nothing to worry about? How do I tell her Norton Valentine is going to end up chasing his own tail? How, Mother, how do I tell her?"

"How do you know Chloe hasn't told him Stopley was here Monday night?"

"She wouldn't."

"How do you know?"

"Because she owes the old man too much."

"You can't scare Chloe, you know that."

"Chloe wouldn't grass."

"I wouldn't be so sure. You didn't see what she was like when she came to see me yesterday. She didn't like what's happened with Viola. She didn't like being interrogated by Sparks. She doesn't like the idea of adverse publicity of any sort. And that gorilla of hers refused a banana." Hagar was on her feet and moving slowly toward the bedroom. She lifted her eyes to a rampart overhead and shuddered. Then she turned, and her eyes met Lila's. "Mr. Valentine has you worried, doesn't he?"

"Any snooper does."

"You tell me he's smart. Much smarter than Mr. Stopley."

"Much."

"In less than twenty-four hours, he's gotten to you, to Karen, to Mickey and Marti, Viola, Chloe . . . and tonight he'll be here."

"Where the trail goes cold."

and swept from the balcony into the bedroom.

Lila clenched her fists and brought them together. Her eyes were misty with tears, and she fought back a sob rising in her throat. The fists unclenched, and her hands wiped at her eyes. She reached for the bottle of beer and gently shook it. The beer foamed, and Lila whispered to the bottle, "I'm glad there's still some life in something around here."

"You said that naughty name, I didn't." Norton crossed a leg and scratched his chest.

"It's a very fashionable name today," said Sparks. "It's big box office. You think Hagar Simon's tied in with them?"

"Or tied to somebody who's tied in with them."

"Maybe those two in the Thunderbird killed Stopley."

"Maybe."

"But you're not ready to buy it."

"I'm not looking for bargains. What're their names?"

"The blond one's Vince Hayes." They heard a chair groan as Gross settled into it. "The redhead's Tom Gucci."

Norton straightened up. "Any relation to Salvatore Gucci?"

"His grandson."

"I thought the Gucci clan went to earth after the old man got exiled back to Italy."

"Tom's a rebel," offered Gross dryly. "He came west about five years ago after his old man had half his head shot off on the front lawn of his house in Hackensack. He was Salvatore's eldest. They never did collar his killer, did they, Ira?"

"Not that I heard," replied Sparks. "Not that anybody cared," he added, "since it didn't trigger off another of their internecine gang wars."

"I know the case well," said Norton. "Just before Cristo Gucci was found dead on his front lawn, there was a rumor going around that he was thinking of making a deal with the government. The big Mafia roundup was on at the time, and Cristo was looking to save his own skin. It was said at the time that old Salvatore back in Italy got wind of it and had his own son fingered."

Sparks smiled. "That sounds like Burton Hartley. The *old* Burton Hartley."

Norton massaged an ear lobe. "Ira, I've got definite proof Clay Stopley was at Hagar Simon's Monday night."

Sparks pulled the cheroot from his mouth. "Karen Frost talked?"

"She's a very capable lady," said Gross.

"Oh, that she is," agreed Norton. "I think she's capable of decoding Stonehenge. I've got a date with her tonight. She's taking me to a party at Hagar Simon's."

"Fast work," said Sparks.

"Faster than I hoped. Too fast," he added cryptically, without elaborating on his personal suspicion that the evening was a hastily put together setup to throw him off the scent, "but I'd like to think Hagar's appetite has been whetted for a taste of me."

"I have to hand it to you, Norton. You draw yourself a straight line and then you follow it."

"Anybody who thinks I'm following a straight line is a square." He embellished the statement with his stupid grin by way of assuring Sparks no offense was intended. "It's how I've always worked, Ira. I charge into every assignment like a bull in a china shop."

"Fox in a chicken coop's more like it," said Gross wryly.

"Anything to stir up a commotion, Boyd. Panic causes confusion, and confusion leads to errors, and I'm beginning to profit." He thought about mentioning Viola Fairbanks's slip about the madras jacket but as quickly realized it could lead to Chloe Jupiter as his informant. He guided them back to Lila Frank. "Lila moves in very strange and very mysterious ways. She was presumably in New York for five days on business, but we happen to know she squeezed in a quick hop to Europe."

Sparks tightened his briefly slack jaw. "Maybe she went there to get laid."

"She's made a great many clandestine trips to Europe over the past three years."

"Collecting news is part of her job, isn't it?" said Sparks.

"Whatever compels her, she's been making an unusual amount of trips abroad. She covers her tracks well. We don't know where she goes."

Boyd suggested, "Maybe you should tie a bell around her neck."

ahead. You want to pull in Tom Gucci and Vince Hayes with charges of suspicion of harassing a private citizen, you do that too. They'll be replaced this fast . . ." he snapped his fingers, and Gross winced, ". . . by another pair of jokers. You said it yourself, Ira. I've accomplished a hell of a lot in a short space of time. I don't know if I'm that smart or that lucky or just another sitting duck. You think I'm not wondering and examining why it is moving all this fast for me? Don't you think I'm suspicious I might be following a trail of carefully laid red herrings? Don't you think I get the cold sweats at the prospect of ending up in Griffith Park as another . . ." he spat each word venomously, ". . . sack of garbage?" He simmered down quickly and reacted with a smile at the puckish expression on Boyd Gross's face. "What's so funny?"

"Your fly's open."

Norton looked down and pulled up his zipper. "I'll have to find me a new tailor." Sparks was at the window with his back to the others, his hands clenched together behind him. It reminded Norton of his father, wondering what punishment to mete out for a youthful peccadillo. He looked at Boyd Gross and shrugged. Gross winked back. Norton felt that in this placid man he might have a friend and an ally. He wished the positions were reversed, with Gross in charge of the investigation of Clay Stopley's murder. It wasn't a matter of distrusting Ira Sparks; it was just that he instinctively knew with Boyd Gross there could be his kind of communication, the kind enjoyed with his superior back in Washington, the kind he used to share with Clay Stopley, regardless of Clay's brief fall from grace after his one-night stand with Marti. Norton shoved his hands in his trouser pockets and began pacing the room slowly. He was searching for the right approach to Ira Sparks. He understood what the man was up against, the feelings of impotence and inadequacy and frustration, possibly even jealousy, emotions that had frequently plagued Norton when caught in a similar situation.

"I know what's rubbing you the wrong way, Ira." Sparks moved his head slightly and saw Norton from the corner of an

"Because we'd have had a second corpse. Either the witness . . . or Clay's killer. All that those frightened guests know is Clay was there and died on the premises. So they've been threatened into this conspiracy of silence. Now there's just one person who might know or suspect what happened to Clay, and that's Karen Frost. I said 'might,' Ira. It's a toss-up why she got that black eye and who delivered the punch. One thing's for sure, she didn't fall off any horse, unless she's got one on rockers in her bedroom."

"We should take her into protective custody," insisted Sparks.

"I'd rather you put a tail on her. Let's find out who visits her or who she's visiting. I don't think she'll be moving out of that apartment very much with that mouse on her eye."

Sparks nodded. "What about Lila Frank . . . Czardi . . . the rest of them . . ."

"I'm just trying to start a little war of nerves. Easiest way to get a structure to shake is to start picking away at the foundations. You'd be surprised how one frightened person can start an epidemic of fear. And frightened people start making all the wrong moves. Czardi, for instance, may not be all that important in this scheme of things, but I've started him sweating. Karen Frost feeds me a bum alibi and then tries to shore it up with an equally feeble assist from this Marti Leigh." He spoke her name hoarsely and covered it by drawing a drink of water from the cooler in the room. "Viola Fairbanks is a dumb little bunny terrified of her aunt. Viola's too dimwitted to know or understand what's going on around her. A paper towel absorbs more. But you don't pigeonhole your dimwits either. Sometimes they make important slips without knowing they've made them." Like madras jacket. "Chloe Jupiter's a tough old bird. She's got one thing going for her the others seem to sadly lack, a great sense of humor. That's what makes her a survivor, and Chloe intends to outlive all of us. So I don't get all that much out of her."

He knew Sparks was swallowing, but how much was he digesting? Had Norton's ears wiggled or his nose twitched

Norton continued. "So little Hagar travels with her mother, obviously a very domineering lady."

"Very," said Sparks after blowing a smoke ring.

"And Hagar gets pushed into a loveless marriage. No back talk. No sass. Just says, 'Okay, Mama, if you want me to marry him, I'll marry him.' But Hagar's a healthy young filly. Where does she get her kicks? Wouldn't you think she might have had some lovers on the side?"

Sparks flicked an ash. "Doesn't everybody?"

"No gossip about her?"

"None I ever heard," said Sparks. "You ever hear of her having any hanky panky, Boyd?"

"Nah, I don't read gossip columns." He smiled at Norton. "That sounds like one for Lila Frank."

"I'm making a mental note." Norton realized he was still holding the empty paper cup, crumpled it, and tossed it into the wastepaper basket. "Well, I better be getting back to the hotel. I've got some phone calls to make. Have we made peace, Ira?"

"Oh, sure," Sparks said lavishly, "you know how it is. Guy's got to let off steam every so often. This isn't the greatest job in the world, you know."

"I know. I don't envy you. And there's them that don't envy me. That's what makes a horse race. I wish I was coming down the stretch."

"Maybe you are, and you don't know it," suggested Gross.

"I'll know it when it's happening. Little bells go off in my head, and they're not the little bells you hear on an ice cream wagon." Gross was out of his chair and following Norton to the door.

"I'm going to grab some lunch, Ira. Be back in half an hour." Sparks grunted. Gross opened the door for Norton. Norton looked at Sparks behind the desk, now busying himself with papers. He thought of saying something by way of farewell, but nothing came to mind, except, "I'll be in touch." Sparks responded with another grunt, and Norton and Gross left.

Hearing the door shut, Sparks looked up. His fist closed

"Ira could use that course in applied psychology."

Gross smiled. "He's jealous of the way you operate. He thinks you're glamorous."

"When next we meet, should I kiss him?"

The waitress arrived on that line and gave Norton a peculiar look. Gross saw the look and chuckled. They ordered chicken sandwiches and coffee, and the waitress departed for the kitchen, after another quick look over her shoulder at Norton. "I think you've just given Sadie the wrong impression."

Norton lifted a sugar cube from Gross's pyramid and tossed it from hand to hand. "You boys should know by now how the secret service works. We're trained to share just so much information and no more. We're also trained to respect the people we work with. I don't know if I like or dislike Ira Sparks, and it really doesn't matter, as long as I'm getting the cooperation I need." He paused to think before making his next statement and then decided to go ahead with it. "Clay Stopley didn't like Ira."

"Didn't like or didn't trust?"

Norton dropped the sugar cube back in the bowl. "You're a smart lad, Gross." He folded his hands on the table and leaned forward. "We've had trouble with the police before. You know law enforcement bureaus resent each other's guts. Everybody's looking for a laurel wreath, even if it's a lousy fit."

"And every time you meet a cop, you're wondering if this is the one that's corrupted."

"That's right. In the sort of organization we suspect Hagar is involved with, corruption is an old and trusted friend. It's like the Dark Ages again, Boyd. There's a new breed of Borgias and Machiavellis. How do I know Hagar's people don't have a pipeline to yours?"

Gross began dismantling his pyramid. "I guess you think it's a gamble breaking bread with me."

"I think it's a gamble every time I use a bathroom."

Sadie was back with the sandwiches and coffee. She had a look of distaste, as though facing the prospect of sharing a to you boys. But I hope the murdering has stopped with Clay."

Boyd's hand holding the coffee cup froze in midair. "You think there might be *more?*"

"I'm always prepared for any eventualities. I was on the team investigating John Kennedy's assassination. There was a chain reaction of very sudden, very mysterious deaths. Some we found out why; some we're still wondering about. It taught me to be prepared. You know that old saw about the Mafia. They only kill each other. Want me to draw pictures where this case is concerned?" He reached into his pocket and withdrew his billfold.

"This tab's mine," protested Boyd. "I invited you."

"I've got a bigger expense account." Norton dropped a bill on the table with an expansive gesture that didn't escape Sadie at the counter. She hastily totaled the tab on her pad and crossed the room with it.

"Will there be anything else?" Sadie's voice betrayed enlarged adenoids.

Norton said with a smile, "Only a worshipful glance." Sadie grabbed the bill from the table and hurried away. Norton broke into Boyd's preoccupation. "Putting a tail on Karen Frost is a very good idea. I hope Ira's following through."

"He's taken care of it by now. Ira may not look it, but he's very thorough. About Lila Frank, I'll start backtracking her. I know you're planning to put your own tracers on her."

"So what? Every little bit helps. I could also use anything you've got on Burton Hartley."

"Off the top of my head, I can tell you he's a lush . . ."

"Fairly common knowledge."

"We've pulled him in on a variety of drunk driving charges, all quashed by someone up there . . ."

"Understandable."

"And for the past couple of years, he's been writing as though somebody's castrated his typewriter."

"He still manages to scoop a couple of juicy plums every

impromptu luncheon invitation? He had to admit to himself, Sparks fascinated him. He was the kind of man who rarely entered Norton's social orbit. He was coarse-hewn and tough, a man whose record carried admirable recommendations. The bureau had checked him out thoroughly. Professional life unblemished. Private life likewise. Private life such as it is.

Hello there! The white Thunderbird was back in his rearview mirror. Now that he knew the names of the two villains, Norton almost felt friendlier toward them. It was still redheaded Tom Gucci at the wheel, and Norton wondered if they ever spelled each other. Were their girlfriends annoyed because they were devoting so much time to Norton? Did they go to church? Were they good to their mothers? Norton almost passed a red light and bore down on the brakes. He heard the screech of brakes behind him and turned around. Vince Hayes had hit his head against the windshield, and it didn't need a lipreader to figure out the imprecations he was mouthing. Gucci was responding with a series of obscene Sicilian gestures. Norton thought the act was almost funny enough to be booked into Las Vegas.

Twenty minutes later, the Renault was parked in the garage under the hotel, and Norton was lying on the couch in his living room talking into the turquoise phone. The monotonous voice coming from the receiver was telling him that Count Miklos Czardi was a bogus nobleman. He had entered the country illegally some thirty years ago. He had led the immigration authorities a merry chase for over two decades before settling in Hollywood and opening his restaurant. Legal action was instigated against him and then quickly and mysteriously dropped. The file on him remained open, however, and if Norton thought it would help to revive the prosecution . . .

"Not yet," interjected Norton sharply. "It may come in handy, but let's keep it in the deep freeze a while longer. Any line on who's been protecting him?" Norton was told the name of an Eastern congressman. It was a familiar name. It

7

"It looked like a very dull day, until I saw you sitting out here."

Norton had changed into violet and yellow swim trunks and had a bath towel casually slung over his right shoulder. He was easing himself into the chaise next to Marti. The fat redhead raised her head for an appraising look at Norton, while Marti made a good show of looking perplexed and wondering who he was.

"Norton Valentine," he said, sounding slighted that anyone could ever forget him. "Last night at Czardi's?"

"Oh, for heaven's sake, of course!" exclaimed Marti in a delectable assortment of vocal tones, "I didn't recognize you without your clothes on." She turned to the fat redhead. "Ella May, this is Norton Valentine." Her neck swiveled back to Norton. "This is my friend, Ella May Rudge."

"Nice to meet you, Ella May."

Ella May's cavern of a mouth opened and shut rapidly like a dolphin contemplating a herring, and then she lazily waved her right hand. "Howary'all, Nawton." There was Blue Ridge Mountains in her voice and pagan lust in her face, and Norton felt like a Christmas turkey.

herself off the chaise. They watched her lumber toward the lobby eagerly, as though answering the mating call of a bull elephant.

"Ella May's such a darling," said Marti mellifluously. "She hasn't been feeling too well since she got here."

"Anthrax?"

"Lay off. She's a nice kid. I met her in London last year when she was doing some p.a.'s. She's got a glorious voice, but unfortunately she's not terribly bright. She still thinks the earth is flat."

"You've certainly been getting around since our late unpleasantness. Hong-King . . . London . . . Hagar Simon's."

"That's me . . . nymph errant. Cigarette?" She reached under her chaise, and a duffel bag materialized. They lit cigarettes and settled back. They sat in silence for a few moments, Norton with so much to ask, not knowing where to begin. Finally he spoke.

"Thanks for not giving the game away last night."

"Save it. They have their suspicions about you."

"I mean about our having been married."

"That was for my own protection. I had to play the game with Clay last Monday night."

"You're slipping. I'm not supposed to know he was there. You were supposed to be in Palm Springs."

Marti flicked an ash and turned to him. "They know you know he was there, and I know you know Palm Springs was a clumsy alibi. Karen never told me which eye got smacked."

They know you know he was there. But how? If Chloe had decided to tell someone she had spilled the beans, why? She'd been adamant that morning about being protected. It couldn't have been Chloe. It had to be something else. Maybe Chloe's house was bugged after all. He'd think about that later. Here was Marti to be dealt with.

"Who smacked Karen in the eye?"

"She hasn't said, but she's plenty frightened."

other before. I was a nervous wreck the whole damned evening."

"Why? What were you afraid of?"

"Oh, stop playing the ass. Don't you think I figured he was at Hagar's on an assignment? Monday wasn't the first time I'd met him there. He'd been there before with Karen and . . ." She caught herself too late.

"So you saw Clay twice. Shall we try for three? Lunch? Cocktails? Did you just happen to be here at the pool one afternoon, and you ran into each other? Come on, Marti. Loosen up those tight lips. Did the two of you toss off a quick one for old time's sake?"

"You *shit*." Her cigarette was almost burnt down to her fingers, and she flung it to the ground with a vehemence, then looked at him with eyes blazing. "I wish I could lie about it just to make you suffer." Anger mercurially gave way to amusement. "Good heavens, Nortie, you're still jealous. Am I having it off with Czardi? Was there another quickie with Clay? Why, Nortie, darling, I'm absolutely flattered. This is your first time at the pool, so that slight tan of yours must have come from the torch you're carrying."

Norton said through clenched teeth, "I'm glad I've made you happy at last." He leaned over and ground out his cigarette butt on the ground without taking his eyes from Marti.

"Don't horse around with me, baby. You're playing with the grown-ups now. You're not posing for Avedon with six layers of gauze over the lens. You're into a lethal situation here, and you'd better start reassessing your priorities. Clay's been murdered. That's no catbird seat your friend Karen's sitting on. You saw Clay a third time, and he trusted you enough to flesh out some of the details of his assignment." *And if he did, and you betrayed him, as much as I still love you, I'll kill you.*

"I saw him at Karen's late Sunday afternoon. She invited me over for a drink. I didn't know he was going to be there.

— 103 —

You want this scene reported to Lila or Hagar or whoever the hell? You think I'd go out of my way to spend time with that sorry tub of lard?" She suddenly laughed graciously, produced her pack of cigarettes, and gaily offered him one. "Smile, dear, we're on 'Candid Camera,' and be a gentleman and light these cigarettes." He took her Zippo and ignited it. Cigarettes aglow, she retrieved the lighter, dropped it in the bag, and set it to one side. "Now then, I'll tell you exactly what I told Clay when I saw him for the *fourth* time." Norton lay back staring at the sky and waited. "We had lunch Monday afternoon. He made a point of inviting both Karen and myself, knowing Karen had a modeling assignment and couldn't make it. And I told him this. I met Czardi at a dinner party in Hong-Kong." She mentioned the name of a Chinese film producer. It sounded like something Norton might have selected from Column A. "I wanted to get back to the States. I was short of cash, and I could see he was interested. Just don't say anything. Just lie there and listen. Yes, I'd been mixed up with somebody, and I wanted out. I told that to Czardi, and my timing was right. I was just what the doctor ordered. He offered me a plane ticket and a bonus to carry a package back here and get it through customs. Presumably it was perfume. Don't say it . . ." He had started to speak, and she was in no mood to be interrupted. "I could figure it out for myself. Heroin, hash . . . whatever. I was desperate enough to gamble and accept the offer.

"Once safely through customs, he paid me off and tried a pass. I politely let him know it was no soap, and he didn't push it. But he did say he knew how I could pick up some more of the green stuff, if I was interested. I was interested. I needed a new wardrobe and a long stay at Main Chance to get back into shape before going to New York to see if I can pick up my modeling career again. He told me about Hagar and how much she pays her girls." She heard his quick intake of breath and said softly, "I promise you, Nortie, I haven't sunk to professional prostitution. I'm just paid to be decoration, be nice to the more important guests from out of town,

"Early the next morning. He phoned. I was still asleep."

"Didn't you ask any questions?"

"Of course, I did!"

"Didn't it occur to you then that Clay might have been dead?"

"I don't know. Maybe it did. I didn't want to think about it. I phoned Karen. She was hysterical. I got dressed and went over to her place."

"Did she have the black eye then?"

Her voice was barely audible. "Yes."

"And she wouldn't say who gave it to her?"

"No."

Something was nagging at Norton's brain. It had to do with Karen Frost, but it wouldn't crystallize. "Have you ever come across two hoods named Tom Gucci and Vince Hayes?" Norton described them.

"No. They don't ring a bell. What about them?"

"They've been on my tail since I got here. They travel in a white Thunderbird. I'm wondering if they provided a similar service for Clay."

"He never mentioned it, if he suspected he was being followed. If he was, then I could be in trouble." Norton was staring at a tub of flowers where three bees were gang-banging a daisy. "Well, *say* something."

"What do you want me to say? Sure, you're in trouble. Whether you and Clay were tailed out to the beach or not, you're in trouble. For starters, you're on Hagar's payroll."

"I can get out of that." There was a crooked smile on her face. "I've disappeared before."

"It won't be that easy this time. You're on file at the bureau now. You know how we operate. Every report I phone in is taped and transcribed. Everything I've accomplished since yesterday, everyone I've met is on the record. Did you expect me not to tell them I've run into my ex-wife? That you knew Clay? That my former beloved is now mixed up in some way with Hagar Simon, and it could give me a headache no aspirin can cure?"

She was stubbing out her cigarette on the ground. "And

Clay." Her voice grew faint. "And not you."

"I guess I'll never figure you out, will I?"

"If I can't, how the hell can you?" Their eyes met, and they both smiled. "I'm a fallen angel, Nortie, a woman no better than she should be, but I still have a few principles. I deliberately set out to have that fling with Clay. I was jealous, and it was childish. You and I were apart so often, I was afraid we'd forget each other's names. I guess I was never meant to be anybody's wife. Anybody's girl, but never anybody's wife."

"I still love you, Marti."

"I guess I know that, Nortie, which makes you a bigger fool than I am. You've got more important things to think about now. There's Hagar, and there's Clay. Don't get sidetracked. It might put you off your guard. I think that's what happened to Clay. I think he was in love with Karen. I think he was spending too much thought on how to protect her. Don't you waste that energy on me." She added airily. "Just try to put in a good word for me, if I ever need it. Now I better go up and go through the motions of my good-byes with Ella May. The poor slob's got a bad back."

"Her front's no better."

Marti laughed. "I'm glad I can still see what I once saw in you, and, buster, that's a compliment. File it for future reference." She walked away, blithely swinging the duffel bag. His eyes followed her until she disappeared into the hotel. He dwelled for a while on what their marriage might have been had either one of them been smarter about managing the other. And then he realized he was wasting precious time.

An hour later, the Renault was parked across the street from Karen Frost's apartment house. Miraculously, there had been no sign of the white Thunderbird from the moment he left the hotel. It almost gave him a feeling of rejection, as though Gucci and Hayes had grown bored with him and decided to catch a movie instead. Or did they know Marti? Had they recognized her when she left the hotel and decided

"I see. Somebody covering the back of the place?"

"Hank Rosen's parked in the garage under the building. There's no back way out. The tenants either come out the front door or go down to the garage. We came out here together."

"Then she's still inside."

"Should be. There was a doorman on when we got here. He said she was in."

"He's not there now."

Grafton shrugged. "He could be any place inside, I guess. I didn't see him go off. Her car's still parked in the garage. It's a Jap job. A red Toyota."

"I've been buzzing her. She doesn't answer."

Grafton shrugged again. "Maybe she vants to be alone."

"Got any keys on you?"

"Always do." Grafton reached into his trouser pockets and handed Norton a set of skeleton keys. Norton returned to the building and buzzed Karen Frost again. He leaned on the bell until the tip of his finger turned white. There was still no response. He let himself into the lobby and looked around for the doorman. There was no sign of life, and the lobby was as silent as a church after mass. He went down the hall past the elevator to Karen Frost's door. He pressed the buzzer there and then banged on the door. He pressed his ear to the door, but heard nothing. He let himself into the apartment.

"Karen?" He shut the door and entered the living room repeating her name. "Karen?" He crossed to the kitchen and then retraced his steps across the living room to the bedroom. He opened the door and went in.

She was lying on the bed in a foetal position. She was wearing a thin housecoat and apparently nothing else. Her eyes were open and milky with death. Her right hand was hidden under her body, but her left was exposed and outstretched. Norton felt for her pulse, knowing it was a vain gesture. There was a scratch mark in the crook of her elbow, as though she might have done battle with an insect or been mainlining. He examined her arm for any telltale syringe

— 111 —

"A little after eight. Why?"

"Did you notice if Miss Frost had any visitors?"

"I don't think so." There was a Latin lilt to the reply. "I mean she might have. I have to go off the post every so often. You know, do an errand for one of the tenants, take a leak, things like that. There's supposed to be two of us on duty, but we're short-staffed, you know?" He regarded Norton quizzically. "Something wrong?"

"Something's wrong." He went outside and waved frantically at Abe Grafton. Grafton left his car and arrived at a sprint. Norton told him about Karen Frost. They entered the building, and Grafton sent the doorman down to the garage to get Hank Rosen. Then he followed Norton back to Karen's apartment. Norton went to the phone while jerking a thumb toward Karen's bedroom. Grafton went there, and Norton dialed Ira Sparks. While he was waiting to be connected, a six-foot cherub entered the apartment, puffing. Hank Rosen had the kind of seraphic face that belonged on a birthday card. He was probably in his late twenties but looked sixteen and unkissed.

"Who're you?" he asked Norton in a piccolo voice that made farce comedy of the stern look on his face.

"Norton Valentine. Grafton's in the bedroom. Karen Frost's dead." Ira Sparks had come on the phone. "Ira? Valentine here. I'm at Karen Frost's. She's dead." Rosen joined Grafton in the bedroom while Norton heard Sparks explode at the other end. "Hold your fire, Ira. Grafton tells me he and his partner only came on an hour ago. She looks and feels as though she's been dead longer than that." He went testy. "No, I didn't grope, but I felt for her pulse, and rigor mortis has set in." He listened. Then he said, "It looks like an overdose of sleeping pills, but I wouldn't say positively. Well . . . her eyes are open. When you o.d. on pills, you usually shut them and go bye-bye. See you soon." He hung up as Grafton and Rosen entered from the bedroom. "Ira's on his way."

Rosen tweetled to Grafton, "He'll chew our asses for this."

emotional a confrontation for a minor matter like that, he thought ironically.

Ella May Rudge.

He reached for the phone and dialed the hotel. He asked for Ella May Rudge. Hank Rosen reacted to her name. "Ella May Rudge, the *singer*. You *know* her?"

Norton was astonished. "Don't tell me you've heard of her?"

"I've got every album she's ever made. She's got the voice of an angel."

"Have you ever seen her?"

"Not in person," said Rosen dreamily.

"Don't, and keep your illusions." Into the phone, he said, "Ella May? Norton Valentine. No, no . . . it's not about a massage . . ." Rosen and Grafton exchanged glances. "I lost Marti's phone number. I was wondering if you had it." She said she'd go look, and he waited. In the distance he could hear the police siren heralding the advent of Sparks and company. The two plainclothesmen got to their feet and busied themselves looking busy. They were badly in need of direction as they renewed looking into closets and drawers. Ella May was back on the phone, and Norton was prepared with address book and pen. She was repeating the number slowly, and he wished somebody was standing behind her with an electric prod. "You're a sweetheart, Ella May. Thanks a million. What? I won't forget. The minute I feel tense, I'll send you a signal. 'Bye now." He hung up as Ira Sparks came charging into the apartment followed by Boyd Gross and Maurice Mosk. Mosk carried his little black bag in his right hand; in his left, he held a pear he was rapidly demolishing. There were no greetings exchanged, although Boyd Gross waved his hand lightly in Norton's direction. Grafton and Rosen led the others to the corpse.

Norton realized this was not the time to phone Marti. Sparks would certainly question why Norton was taking special pains to alert her.

"What brought you here this time?" He hadn't heard

Ira, but I guess it was a little too late."

Sparks was wiping sweaty palms with a bandanna handkerchief. "That's what stinks about this job. Not enough men available. It took 'em over an hour to round up Grafton and Rosen." He stopped Mosk who was heading through the living room toward the front door. "Maurice, how long would you say she's been croaked?"

"About two to three hours, maybe longer. I'll know better later." He continued out.

Sparks said to Norton, "Any chance you're going to tell me what you were going to ask Frost?"

"Sure," said Norton. "I was going to ask her if she saw Clay Stopley murdered."

"What makes you think she did?"

"Her black eye, among other things." He headed for the door. He glanced at his wristwatch and said, "I'll phone you later for the autopsy report. Oh, by the way, I seem to have lost Tom Gucci and Vince Hayes. You didn't warn them off me by any chance?"

Sparks stuck his thumbs in his belt. "You told me it wasn't worth the bother."

"I know. But I wondered if they might have been called off me long enough to take care of Miss Frost." The attendants were crossing the room, carrying the covered stretcher.

Sparks said, "I'll ask them about that." He spoke to Gross. "Have them brought in." Gross crossed to the telephone to dial headquarters. Norton followed the stretcher-bearers into the hall. He didn't for one moment think that the two hoods were responsible for Karen Frost's death, but he thought the suggestion to Sparks might meet with Boyd Gross's approval. The doorman held open the door for the morgue attendants. Norton spoke to the man as he passed him. "Better let your bosses know there's another apartment available."

derer might have an additional cast of characters to worry him. Karen either saw the murder committed or had a pretty fair guess as to the identity of the killer. The killer was taking no chances on her promised silence under the duress of a beating and eliminated her. Karen must have an address book or possibly a diary, and there was no sign of either at her apartment. He voiced all this to Ira Sparks, who surfaced from his reverie with a troubled look.

"I been thinking along the same lines," said Sparks gruffly. "Now, if I could find out who Karen Frost's been buddy-buddy with . . ."

"Stands to reason they be among Hagar Simon's regulars."

"Stands to reason, all right." He was agitating his hands against his thighs. Gross wondered if it was only these murders troubling him. "I'm almost tempted to subpoena Valentine for the information he's withholding."

"Fat lot of good that would do you. His L.A. office would kill it before the ink was dry."

"I'd like to beat it out of him. Don't give me one of your tender looks. That's how I feel, and I don't give a dead hump who knows it. I know, I know . . . if Stopley hadn't been a Fed, the case would have been left to us. But he was a Fed, and the Feds look after their own. Well, Karen Frost was just a plain civilian, and she belongs to us. Let little Norton try to stick his two cents in where *she's* concerned." He now sat with his arm across the back of the seat behind Boyd Gross. "You like that bastard, don't you?"

"Valentine? What's to dislike?"

"I mean, you admire him." The challenge in Sparks's voice spelled trouble. Boyd Gross wondered if he dared crash into the car ahead of them. "Well, you do, don't you?"

"Is it illegal?"

"I didn't ask for any smartass lip. What's to admire in him?"

"He's not afraid to die."

Sparks detonated. "That's a reason to admire him? You afraid to die? Am I afraid to die?"

— 119 —

"I didn't know till I got back. There was a message to call Czardi. I can cancel if you prefer."

"Don't cancel. I like having you where I can keep an eye on you."

"Now, Norton, have you any real reason to think I might be in danger?" She was working too hard on a jocular tone. Norton could sense she was frightened.

"Do you know if Karen kept a diary?"

"I don't. She might have. Why?"

"I frisked her place before calling the police. No address book, no letters. No ashes in either of her fireplaces. Maybe there was a diary, and maybe there wasn't. But an address book had to exist, and I should think she would have had a date book."

"She did have that. She was always making a note of appointments. She always scribbled down who she saw and when she saw them."

"Let's hope she was too upset at the time to scribble you down for Tuesday morning."

"Thanks for the kind thought." The line seemed to go dead.

"*Marti?*"

"I'm here. I'm here. I was just thinking about something. She probably has some family someplace, but I haven't the vaguest idea where . . . I mean . . . what about her funeral? Who'll take care of that?"

"Perhaps Hagar will do the right thing."

"That's almost funny."

"Don't worry about it now. It'll be in the newspapers tomorrow. Some relative might spot it and come forward. Marti, I want you to spend some time thinking hard about Tuesday morning at Karen's. Anything you remember she told you. *Anything*. Some hint, some little description of the bastard who hit her. That's who killed her. That's who killed Clay." He wanted to add, but didn't: And that's who might try to kill you and a dumb little bunny named Viola Pickfair, who spent time with Karen Frost yesterday. And anybody got to her feet slowly. "Uh'll send muh boys for Viola immediately. Anybody harms a hair of her head will have tuh answer tuh me puhsonally. Uh'll blow the whole works. Gimme the name of yuh hotel. Uh'll be in touch if there's any problem." She listened for a moment. "Yuh'll be at Hagar's later. Make a note of that, Horace. Norton, yuh look out for yuhself. Yuh playin' with fire. Uh don't want yuh tuh get singed in the wrong places." She hung up. "Horace! Get a couple of the boys up from muh puhsonal gymnasium in the basement and go get Viola and bring her here. Make shuah she packs an overnight bag. And, Irvin', put that solid gold string back in muh jewel case 'n' go outside 'n' jog."

Norton phoned Ira Sparks, but was told he was out of the office. He asked for Boyd Gross and was finally connected with him in the morgue. He told him of the possible danger to Marti and Viola. "Viola's aunt is moving her out to her place. She'll be safe there."

"I'll put Grafton onto Marti Leigh," said Boyd. "I've got the autopsy report on the Frost girl. You were right. She didn't o.d. There wasn't enough nembutal in her to kill her. There were traces in her mouth, throat and lungs, which indicates whatever she imbibed was forced into her. She was killed by an air bubble. An empty syringe injected into the crook of her left elbow. The shock was instant and killed her."

"Christ," whispered Norton. "Has Sparks heard this report?"

"Not yet. He's out of the office on something else. Tom Gucci and Vince Hayes haven't been picked up yet either. We're having a very bad day around here."

"Sometimes bad days turn out to be the best."

"Maybe for you." He lowered his voice. "Sparks is on the warpath. You may find him a bit troublesome from here on in."

"I was expecting it. It'll be handled. Please get after Abe Grafton. Marti's at the Malibu Mistral. I spoke to her half an hour ago. Then she's being escorted to Hagar Simon's tonight an inquisitive canary, anxious to find out why Marti was telling whoever it was she was speaking to that Viola was afraid of heights. Viola was afraid of a lot of things from the moment Marti had told her Karen Frost was dead. She was afraid of her aunt and the police and Norton Valentine and why Marti had been pressing her to try and remember as much as possible of her conversation with Karen yesterday.

Marti now knew Viola was another potential victim. She was listening to Norton suggest off the top of his head that she accompany Viola to Chloe Jupiter's. He would call the police station and have Boyd Gross apprise Abe Grafton of Marti's destination. He'd get back to Chloe and tell her to expect both women.

"Well, if you say so, I suppose it's as good an alternative as taking it on the lam," Marti said to Norton halfheartedly.

"You'll be perfectly safe at Chloe's. Now the two of you get moving."

"Wait a minute! I have to tell Czardi!"

"Do it fast, and for God's sake, get a move on!"

Marti winced at the sound of the phone being slammed on the receiver at the other end. She replaced hers and snapped her fingers at Viola. "On your toes, Viola, we're going to your Aunt Chloe's."

"Aunt Chloe? Was that Aunt Chloe you were talking to? Has she asked us to dinner and maybe she's invited a lot of important people who could help me in my career . . ."

She cascaded onward, while Marti wished she had a suture for the chatterbox's mouth.

"Well, what are you packing all that stuff for? Are you spending the weekend? I didn't know you were that friendly with Aunt Chloe because Aunt Chloe doesn't have any women friends not because she doesn't like women but she says most of the women in this town belong to car pools and who are you phoning *now*?"

Norton was busy on his phone to relay the necessary information to Chloe Jupiter and Boyd Gross. He spoke to Chloe first.

out of his trousers and flung them on a chair. Abe Grafton would have to suffer the wild goose chase out to Marti's hotel. He hoped Marti and Viola were on their way to Chloe's. His wristwatch told him there was still a little time to spare before showering and dressing to get to Lila Frank's by eight. He switched on the television set, and into view flicked a grandfatherly gentleman exhorting the elderly to avail themselves of his cut-price dental service. Norton lit a cigarette and tried to compose his thoughts.

There was so much nagging at his brain. His built-in shrew of logic was scolding away, exhorting him to find the logical progression of the clues he had that would lead him to the murderer. Things he had seen, things he had heard and filed away in his brain, little nuggets crying for refining and polishing, to be strung together into a fatal noose. There was too much sidetracking him. Karen's murder. The threat of death hanging over Marti and Viola. Ira Sparks's growing animosity toward him. His top priority should be the cracking of the Hagar Simon assignment. But his instinct was also telling him these parallel lines would suddenly verge and meet at a common junction. Both cases would fuse and explode together. Karen Frost's death might be a blessing in disguise. It could cause a chain reaction that might detonate in his favor. A firework lighting up the sky and spelling out the answers. What was it he knew that was more important than he realized when he heard it?

What the hell's that carnival absurdity on the television screen? The soundtrack was blaring "The Saber Dance," and a beautiful comet wearing the briefest of costumes of spangles and rhinestones and peacock feathers was flashing across a frozen lake wearing shocking pink ice skates. Her hands were gracefully outstretched as she pirouetted into the air and performed a *tour jeté* that brilliantly dissolved into a breath-catching arabesque. She landed on the tips of her skates and held a pose that was caught in closeup by an adoring cameraman, and Norton remembered here was Hagar Holt Simon at the height of her beauty. Then there was a quick cut

"Oh, go away, Lila. Go away, and ponder your sins. Do anything you like. I'm out of this. This morning I did the bravest act of my life. I tendered my resignation to the newspaper."

"Burton!"

"I sent a carbon copy to our syndicate. I am now composing my farewell column. I am using prose more purple than my past. Like an old general, I am fading away. I am finished. Kaput. I thought this out carefully in a briefly sober moment in my bath this morning, and for the first time without the fear of someone pulling the plug. I ate a lavish lunch at Scandia without fear of indigestion and washed it down with a piquantly presumptuous bottle of California claret."

"Why didn't you talk this over with me first?" She was flinging her mules at the dogs.

"In a way, I was trying to do that last night. But somehow, it came out all wrong. You've become much too intimidating, Lila. Your fanatical single-mindedness leaves room for nothing else. You've even forgotten we once shared what I look back upon as a rather delightful grand passion."

"That was no grand passion!" Her eyes were ablaze, and her nostrils flared. The dogs had each retrieved a mule and now begged at her feet for a reward, with tails wagging. "It wasn't even good. It just killed time."

He said softly, "I prefer to remember it my way. Now perhaps we should hang up. Hagar may be trying to get through to you."

"I wish I could get through to *you*."

"You have. Believe me, you have." He hung up.

"Burton! *Burton!*" Furiously, Lila jiggled the hook. "Burton, don't you dare hang up on me!" The dogs were whining for attention. "You monsters!" She slammed the phone down and began chasing the dogs around her bedroom. "You know what those goddamn mules *cost?!*"

Marti's hands were tight on the wheel of her yellow

Norton left the television set on as he carried his drink into the bathroom. He set it down on the sink and tested the hot water in the shower. When he adjusted it to a suitable temperature, he took a sip of the drink, stuck his tongue out at himself in the mirror, then set the drink down again, and removed his undershorts. He stepped under the shower, reached for the soap, and began working up a lather. The music from the television set suddenly increased in volume, and Norton decided another of Hagar's production numbers was underway. He soaped his body and face vigorously and neither heard nor saw the door to the shower stall opening.

In a shockingly swift movement, a towel was flung around his face nearly suffocating him. He dropped the soap and lifted his hands in a lightning movement, but the lightning never had a chance to strike. His hands were grasped and pulled behind him in an agonizing grip. A kick to his ankle sent an electric pain through his system, and his knees buckled. He received a sledgehammer blow to his kidney and then another and then another, and he could not cry out because the towel around his head muffled any sound he tried to make. Blow after blow battered his torso as the shower water poured down on him. Then the door slid shut, and he collapsed to the floor of the stall. The towel now draped limply, and Norton began to retch.

Viola was paralyzed with fear. Her mouth was agape but her vocal chords were frozen. Marti was maneuvering desperately to keep the convertible in control. The red Toyota was trying to force her off the road. The maniac behind the wheel of the Toyota had the brim of his fedora pulled down masking the upper portion of his face. *Why doesn't a car come from the opposite direction. Please God, send a car from the opposite direction!*

God heard. He sent a car from the opposite direction, just as Marti went hurtling around a curve. The driver of the other car, a pickup truck, was caught unawares. He looked like a teenage boy barely old enough to hold a license. That

9

Hagar Simon, toilette completed, was returning Lila Frank's phone call. She was swathed from shoulders to ankles in a bouffant dressing gown of white egret feathers. She gave the impression of having been submerged in a snow bank. Her face was heavily oiled with a miracle lotion that promised eternal, wrinkle-free beauty. She might have been bobbing for apples in a tub of vaseline. She sat at her dressing table, delicately balancing in her left hand the receiver of a beige-colored Princess telephone. While she was dialing, her eyes were glued to the reflection in the mirror of a portable television screen. She held an amused expression, as she watched herself skating rapidly and frantically on a frozen river. The soundtrack underlined the urgency of her situation with the *William Tell Overture*. She was being pursued by six Nazi officers in a snowmobile. Ahead of her lay the precipice of a frozen niagara. Bullets whizzed past her ears, while one of the Nazi officers, possibly a devotee of Herman Melville, was poised and taking aim with a rather sophisticated-looking harpoon. Somehow in the midst of this peril, Hagar found the audacity to perform a series of exquisite pliés.

and the pain began to ease. "Where will you go? What will you do?"

"Why the hell do I have to go anyplace? I'm staying right here. Nobody's got a thing on *me*. I'm in the clear. I'm perfectly *safe*."

How lucky for you, thought Hagar. How very lucky for you. It's only pawns like Hagar Simon who get moved around the board and then knocked out of the game. Lila was continuing to make noises. "Lila, you're wasting time. We both have a lot to do."

"For God's sake, tell me who killed Stopley!"

"I can't. I won't."

"Putana!"

"Call me a whore. Call me anything you like. But one day soon you'll understand why I didn't tell you. And don't labor the issue at the party. You do, and I'll blow the lid off." Lila's invective scorched Hagar's ear. "You heard me!" shouted Hagar. "My deal promised me protection, and by God, I mean to have it. Now get off the phone, and do your job!" She hung up and fumbled with a bottle of nitroglycerine tablets. She popped two in her mouth and waited for the medication to take effect. She could feel the blood returning to her face as she reached for the house phone and pressed a button. It connected to a sentry box. "It's Mrs. Simon. Listen carefully. I want you to double-check every guest against the list I've given you. No one, do you understand, no one is to be admitted to the grounds, unless they can give satisfactory identification." She switched her finger to another button. It connected with the garage. "This is Hagar. Now listen carefully, darling. Fill the tank of my fastest car. Pack something for yourself. Only what's necessary. Don't ask questions. Just do as I tell you. Be ready to leave on a moment's notice. When the party is underway, come to my suite and take my brown suede case down to the car. *Make sure you're not seen*. And, darling, don't forget your passport. Well, where do you think we're heading? South, darling, along with the rest of the birds." She pressed a third

He took another deep breath and then pulled himself up. Oh, Jesus, what agony! His head began to spin, and he braced himself against the wall. He blinked his eyes rapidly until they focused properly. He shook his head and then exhaled. He took a tentative step and then another, and the pain was nowhere near what he anticipated. He'd be all right. He'd make it fine. He wrapped a towel around his midriff and slowly entered the sitting room. He lowered himself gingerly onto the couch and stared at the sliding door he had pushed back earlier when the room overheated. Smart old Norton. Clever old Norton. Always make it easy for the opposition to come in and beat you up. Ah, dear old Ira Sparks. How you would enjoy this moment. How that craggy face would be wreathed with a smile of self-satisfaction. Well, you deserve it, you dirty old mothergrabber.

Norton found his cigarettes and lighter. He lit up and inhaled and then blew a smoke ring and answered the persistent ringing of the hotel phone. It was Boyd Gross.

"Sorry I took so long getting back to you. I was out getting something to eat."

How nice to know the outside world still functions normally. People still eat. People get murdered. People get beaten up. Business as usual. Even Norton's voice sounded normal to himself. Things were looking up. He told Boyd about sending Marti and Viola to Chloe Jupiter's. Boyd said he'd get a motorcycle cop to alert Grafton. Abe was using his own car. It wasn't equipped with a radio phone. Boyd agreed the girls might be safer with Viola's glamorous aunt. Norton then told him about the beating. Gross reacted with comforting concern. Norton assured him he'd be in shape to accompany Lila Frank to Hagar's party. Not to worry, Boyd, he wouldn't miss it for the world. Yes, said Boyd, Gucci and Hayes were still eluding the dragnet, so undoubtedly they could very well have been the culprits.

"Frost's apartment has been thoroughly dusted and sealed," added Gross. "So far nothing useful, but forensics is staying with it. It'll be on the late television news and in insulin into his thigh. Then he leaned with both hands on his desk, waiting for the trembling to stop. He gulped air and wiped his brow with a jacket sleeve. He adjusted his trousers and sat in the swivel chair. He replaced the syringe in its case and put it inside his jacket pocket. He was lighting a cheroot when Boyd Gross knocked on the door and entered.

"Christ, I'm glad you're back."

"Nice to know I was missed. I was beginning to think the department could run itself."

Gross ignored the sarcasm and launched into a detailed report of the events concerning Marti Leigh and Viola Pickfair. Sparks listened with a variety of expressions, none of them pleasant. He cursed himself aloud for having taken the time to see his doctor for a checkup. He cursed the municipal government for providing insufficient funds for the required manpower. He ordered an escalation in the search for Tom Gucci and Vince Hayes and an all-points alert for Marti Leigh and Viola Pickfair. Gross had a strange expression on his face.

"What the hell's the matter with you?" roared Sparks.

"Just thinking of my wife, that's all," said Gross, swiftly. "She'll have to eat another lonely dinner."

"Tough on her!"

Gross returned to his office and phoned Norton. Norton was dressed and ready to leave to pick up Lila Frank. Norton was grateful for Gross's information, and on one point, more than grateful. He rewarded Gross with the inside information of the plan evolved by Norton's local office for later that evening. "It blows tonight," concluded Norton. "It's earlier than scheduled, but it blows. We've got no choice. If anything new turns up, you certainly know where to reach me."

Norton phoned Chloe. He was only able to reassure her the police had ordered the all-points alert for Marti and Viola. Chloe wasn't satisfied. "Uh'm gonna call the governor 'n' get the National Guard. He owes me a favor, y'know." Norton tried to assure her such drastic measures weren't necessary. He asked her to keep in touch with him at

"I suppose we're the first," crackled the old sparrow.

Hagar went to them with outstretched hands and a professional smile. "Margot darling! You're the first and the most welcome. And Manuel, how dashing you look!" Manuel flashed his ivories as he took one of Hagar's hands and kissed it. The majordomo signaled past the group to someone in the great banquet hall, and a Brahms string quartet flooded the castle from carefully hidden speakers.

Margot parted her shriveled lips and whispered to Hagar, "It's our anniversary. Two weeks today since I brought Manuel up from Tiajuana."

Hagar thought to herself, and they said it wouldn't last.

Perched on a leather stool at the bar in her living room, Lila Frank was cooling her right index finger in a glass of champagne. The digit ached from the excessive amount of dialing she had accomplished since speaking to Hagar. Her vocal chords ached from the shouting they'd been subjected to, but she felt satisfied and confident. Only one call had come through on her private wire, and the news it brought her had filled her with apoplectic fury.

"I told you no rough stuff, you bloody bastard! Since when have you started making your own decisions? So you don't like his face. All right, all right, so I told you not to lay a finger on him! Ahhhhh, you're dumb like the rest of them! Dumb, I tell you, *dumb!*" She then spewed a stream of gutter invective followed by, "Well, you at least had the sense to ditch the car. What do you want for that? A gold star? Where you calling from? Uh huh, that's at least using your head. Well, stay there, and I'll call you later. Listen! *Wait!* He ain't *dead*, is he? *Mama mia*, thank God for that. Do you realize now this whole goddamn affair at Hagar's is a big expensive waste of time? Ahhhh, go stick your head up a pig's ass!"

She glanced at her wristwatch and drained the champagne from the glass. She hopped off the stool and adjusted her red and gold sari. The things she let Jean Louis talk her into. She hope you don't mind, but we'll have to make an early night of it. I've got a heavy day tomorrow, starting at the crack of dawn. I tape my television show."

"Fine by me. I don't know how long this back of mine will hold up."

"You poor guy. You should have seen a doctor."

"If I don't feel any better in the morning, I'll see one."

"Awful about Karen."

"Awful."

"How'd you hear about it?"

"I found her body."

Lila stared at him. "You have a date with her?"

"No, I just decided to drop by and ask her a few more questions."

Lila settled back in the seat. "You're not really a stock-broker, are you?"

"Not really."

"You a private investigator or something?"

"I'm doing Clay's family a favor. We've known each other a long time. Clay and I were at college together. He was the best man at my wedding."

Don't be dead, Marti. Please don't be dead. It's all I can bear being haunted by Clay. Don't be dead, because I love you, and I want you back. I'm a damn fool to want you back, but that's how it is. I want you back.

"Seems to me you said in the plane you weren't married."

"We were divorced a couple of years ago."

"Why the stockbroker act?"

"People are less suspicious when you're hunting information and invitations. I know Clay was murdered at Hagar's castle."

"You've got positive information?"

"Very positive."

"Who from?"

"That would be telling."

"That's why I'm asking. Don't forget I'm a reporter."

"Heard any good reports lately?"

On Malibu Canyon Road, where the accident between Marti's yellow Chrysler convertible and the pickup truck had taken place, Horace X.'s motorcycle was now parked. He had come across the telltale skid marks. Now, scrambling down to the valley below in his white jumpsuit and matching white helmet, he looked like a black ghost. The pickup truck was burnt out but still smoldering. In the glare of his flashlight, he saw Marti's upended car. His feet struck rocks and shale causing clouds of dust and a mini-avalanche. He directed his flashlight at the pickup truck. What was behind the wheel looked like a side of charred beef. He swung the flashlight around and saw the doors had been torn loose from the other car. The tree it had connected with was almost uprooted. There was nobody behind the wheel. The body in the passenger seat hung limply, held in place by a safety belt. Horace X. reached the car and recognized Viola. From the angle of her head he could tell her neck was broken. She was heavily cut and bruised, and her face and body was caked with blood. Horace X. cursed aloud and then went looking for the driver. He found Marti some twenty feet away from the car sprawled on her back across some clumps of chapparal. She wasn't a pleasant sight. Blood and dirt almost totally obscured her features. From the way her legs were twisted, Horace X. could tell they were badly broken. He knelt at her side and touched a hand. It was warm. He listened for a heartbeat and heard a faint response. No one had ever scrambled up that ravine with the speed and desperateness displayed by Horace X.

"I've heard so much about you, Mr. Valentine."

Norton held Hagar in his eyes. He was unprepared for the delicate beauty of the lady in person. Here was no steely-eyed harpie, no Medusa to turn him to stone. It was hard for him to believe this soft and voluptuous woman who was greeting him with warmth and friendliness had caulked the seams of her middle-age with corruption and immorality. He would have cast her as the headmistress of an elegant girl's

"Magnificent tapestries," commented Norton.

Lila was caught in the middle of a loud greeting across the vast room to Margot and Manuel. "The Gobelins will get you if you don't watch out."

"It's been said before," replied Norton drily. Scanning the crowded room, he was reminded of a painting by Breughel. Walpurgis night in southern California. Hagar, the stunning witch who probably wouldn't know the difference between a broomstick and a vacuum cleaner. Her hastily assembled guests, extras, bit players and walk-ons, a bizarre potpourri of decadents and innocents, greedily swilling her free liquor and stripping the buffet tables like a plague of destructive beetles. Gossip masquerading as wit, innuendo trespassing as bon mots; gone was a gentler era when ladies dropped their handkerchiefs instead of their brassieres. His innards recoiled with disgust at the sight of shriveled Margot and her young Mexican consort in a kiss so passionate their eyeballs were touching. The music now blaring from the hidden speakers was atonal and existential and offended him with its dissonance, and Lila was tugging impatiently at his sleeve.

"Some party!" she shouted.

"Wow."

"I didn't think you were very impressed." She sipped her drink. "Did Harvey Tripp really hang himself?"

"From a flagpole outside his window. I'm told a dozen people saluted before they realized it was a body."

"Why didn't you tell me about his suicide on the plane?"

"I didn't want you worrying Hagar."

Her eyebrows went up. "Why should it worry Hagar?"

"There's a lot about her in his private papers."

They were standing near open French doors leading to a garden, and a light breeze sent some strands of Lila's hair fluttering across her face. She brushed them aside with a gesture of annoyance, as she said, "I gather you've been privy to those papers."

Norton's smile was not a friendly one. "Why else would I mention them?"

"Maybe to start a little panic around here."

could see Miklos Czardi and Burton Hartley and caught a quick glimpse of Hagar conferring with a butler, but neither of the three noticed her. She trilled a ridiculous laugh and said, "So I've got a boyfriend stashed away over there. Very important. Very famous. Very married. So we have to make elaborate plans to meet on the sly, that's a Federal case?"

"It might be if the boyfriend's Salvatore Gucci."

"Who?" She repeated the ridiculous laugh. "You got rocks in your head, you know that? Where would I know Salvatore Gucci? He's an old man! I was a kid when he was deported! Ah, come on now, Norton. Don't disappoint me. I thought you were smarter than that. So you've had a tracer on me because Stopley met me at one of Hagar's parties. Whatever you boys think you've got on Hagar, anybody who knows her is suspect. Okay, I buy that. Guilt by association. What the hell! Why would this party be put up special for you? Why would I have you beaten up?"

"This party *was* put on special for me, because there was no party planned when you invited me last night. There's a tight security on all of Hagar's regulars. They didn't get any invitations until this morning by phone. Tom Gucci is Salvatore's grandson. I think you know Tom Gucci."

"Never met him in my life." She snarled the sentence like a cornered cat.

"Okay, if that's the way you want it."

"I'm telling it like it *is*."

"You're telling it the way you'd like it to be. I'm telling you you're a liar, and you ought to listen to my deal."

She told him to do something to himself that was physically impossible.

"Not with my bruised ligaments, honey. Lila . . . Harvey Tripp's papers . . . you're mentioned in them. Prominently."

"So *that's* Norton Valentine. He's not at all the way I pictured him. He's handsome enough, but hardly heroic. But then, in these dreadful times, heroes and villains are so interchangeable, it's the era of the chameleon. I want to talk to him. I want to hear more about Harvey Tripp. I've still a few more columns to deliver. I'd love to leave my readers with one last blaze of glory. Doesn't Lila look frantic? I wonder if she made the mistake of asking him to guess her age."

They elbowed their way past two women discussing a celebrated local gigolo.

"I despise that man," said one woman. "He's always taking money from women."

"So is Ohrbach's."

They recognized Czardi and gurgled in his direction. He blew kisses and then averted his face with a grimace.

Lila was saying with defiance to Norton, "I never said ten words to Harvey Tripp!"

"Nine was enough."

"Lila, my darling, we've been looking all over for you!" Czardi wedged himself between Lila and Norton and threw his arms around her and their cheeks brushed. "You look ravishingly exotic. You belong in Taj Mahal with a sultan at your feet." Norton wondered if Lila was wishing a magic carpet would materialize. "And Mr. Valentine. How nice to see you again. I don't believe you've met Burton Hartley." Hartley transferred his drink to his left hand and gave Norton a wet handshake.

"Glad to meet you, Mr. Hartley. I've been looking forward to it."

"I hear you bear sad tidings of Harvey Tripp. A most disagreeable person, Mr. Tripp. I can't believe he hung himself. Surely he died of satyriasis."

"No, he hung himself from a flagpole with a sashcord. Imported, of course."

"Tell them about his papers, Norton," interjected Lila shrewishly. "Or did Tripp omit fingering these boys?"

Norton flagged a passing waiter carrying a tray of drinks and selected a scotch and water. He saw Hartley's Cheshire-cat grin. But he knew this time the smile would soon fade, and the cat would remain. "No pursuit, Mr. Valentine?"

"She won't get very far."

"As far as she needs to get, Mr. Valentine, which is the most convenient house telephone. The lesser two of Lila's necessary evils are hidden in my house. I believe they paid you a visit earlier this evening. Tom Gucci and Vince Hayes." Norton set his glass on a table. "But the remainder, a very large remainder, are scattered throughout Hagar's castle. They'll be troublesome. Whatever it is you're supposed to do, Mr. Valentine, I think you ought to do it."

"Mr. Hartley, I can't wait to find out why you decided to blow it for me."

"Oh, I've spent the whole day writing it, Mr. Valentine. It's all locked in my private safe. I made the futile gesture of resigning from an organization, an organization to which I have been of very minor use of late. But they don't like resignations. I only showed up tonight because I knew you'd be here. And I suspected you had every intention of rocking the boat. I'm asking for a lifesaver, Mr. Valentine."

"Thank you. I'll do the best I can." Norton strolled away and into the garden.

Czardi was mopping his brow. "They can't touch me. I have diplomatic immunity." Hartley snorted. From the garden, they heard two revolver shots.

Horace X. heard the police and ambulance sirens, and from around the curve ahead of him, he saw the reflection of headlights. His motorcycle was propped up against his thigh, and he held tightly to the handlebars, ready to straddle the seat, gun the motor, and deliver the tragic tidings of Viola's death to Chloe Jupiter. From behind him blended the additional sounds of a motorcycle and an automobile. He turned and saw the arrival of a motorcycle cop and Abe Grafton. As the cop and Grafton left their vehicles, the

Gross. "Take care of this!" shouted Gross. "There's a May Day at Hagar Simon's!"

Hagar Simon had changed into a black pantsuit and was opening her wall safe when she heard the revolver shots from the garden. She could feel the hairs rising on the nape of her neck as her face colored with apprehension. She worked the safe dial frantically and was oblivious to the sound of the door opening behind her. She pulled the safe door open and was reaching in to claim her treasures when Lila's rasping voice froze her. "Where the hell do you think *you're* going?"

Hagar spun around and saw Lila advancing on her menacingly. "I'm getting out. And don't you try to stop me." Her hand shot back into the safe like a greedy child given the run of a candy store. Lila lunged at her and dragged her away from the safe. Hagar's hand connected heavily with Lila's cheek. Lila bellowed in pain and outrage as she staggered back. Hagar rushed to her dressing table and tugged at the drawer containing the snub-nose automatic. Lila leapt on her back, her fingers clawing at Hagar's throat. Hagar gasped and sank to her knees, her hand now groping desperately on the tabletop for her heavy Louis XV hand mirror. Lila released one hand and grabbed for Hagar's wrist. Hagar heaved, and her body shot back like an angry mule's. Lila grunted and fell backwards. Hagar grabbed the hand mirror, staggered to Lila with the hand clutching the mirror upraised, and then struck her with brutal force on her left temple. Lila's eyes showed white as she went limp. Hagar fought for breath as she moved back against the dressing table. She could feel a thousand pinpricks as she clutched her breast. She doubled over, catching a glimpse of her unbecoming disarray in the dressing table mirror, and then edged her hand toward her bottle of nitroglycerine tablets. She thought of her handsome, muscular chauffeur and mewled pathetically. For the first time in years, she wished the late Isaac Simon was in the room with her to order a retake of the scene.

· · ·

wondering what the hell was keeping Hagar.

At the entrance to the estate, the sentries had been rounded up by several Feds and were being frisked, as a dozen other government men advanced on the castle.

From the heart-shaped balcony adjoining her boudoir, Chloe was watching the chaos at the castle through her pair of high-powered binoculars. In her bedroom, Irving the gorilla reluctantly left the television set and Bette Davis in *The Sisters* to join Chloe. In Chloe's garden and on her front lawn there was gathered a motley assortment of her retainers, former pugilists and wrestlers, dotted with a quartet of promising muscle men who inhabited the heart-shaped gymnasium and living quarters behind her pink house. Horace X. came roaring down the road and into the driveway. Chloe snapped her fingers at Irving the gorilla, and he followed her from the balcony into the bedroom and from there to her private heart-shaped elevator, which took them with dispatch to the floor below.

At the entrance to the castle, Ira Sparks arrived with two other squad cars, his eyes and face ablaze with anger at his authority being superseded. His loathing for Norton Valentine boiled at having been kept in ignorance of the planned federal raid.

In the blue salon of the castle, four people of apparent wealth and breeding were engrossedly engaged in a bridge game.

"Two no trumps!" blared East.

"Pass," said North glumly.

"Pass," said West sweetly, and East threw his cards in his wife's face.

In the grand hallway, Miklos Czardi held tightly to the arms of two women, trying desperately to camouflage himself between them as he guided them outside.

"But I don't want to leave!" cried one of the women, a blowsy blonde who slapped feebly at Czardi's hand.

strains of "The Lass with the Delicate Air." He passed Miklos Czardi futilely arguing with a federal agent. Inside the castle, Burton Hartley had found a telephone and was slurring a report on the bedlam to the night editor of his newspaper. The old juices were at a boil, and he felt young again. In this brief moment, he relived the triumphs of his youth as a callow reporter making his first scoop. This would be his last, and he treasured every moment of it. The night editor at the other end couldn't understand a word he was saying and was tearing at his sideburns with frustration.

The nitroglycerin tablets had revived Hagar to the extent that she was able to fill her jewel case hastily and pick her way past Lila Frank, lying prone on the floor, to a panel in the wall beyond her canopied bed. The panel was embossed with a fresco of Apollo, whose navel she pressed, and the wall panel slid back revealing a hidden passage. Lila groaned and began to revive. Her eyes fluttered open, and she felt her throbbing temple and the warm blood seeping from the wound. She struggled to her knees and saw Hagar disappear into the hidden passage and the panel slide shut behind her. "Putana!" gasped Lila, as she reached for a bed poster and pulled herself to her feet.

In the cavernous hallway outside, Norton was rushing from door to door in search of Hagar's bedroom. In some of the rooms, he saw Hagar's men tearing out fixtures and smashing false wall mirrors that revealed hidden rooms and cameras. Norton's own men were now converging, and he directed them toward their quarry. He rounded a corner and collided with Ira Sparks. Sparks's face contorted with recognition and hatred. Norton shouted, "Find Hagar Simon!" Sparks's gun hand shot out and connected with Norton's face. Norton staggered backward and caught himself from falling by grabbing the grillwork of an iron door that lead to one of the turrets. Sparks's foot shot out and caught Norton in the thigh. Norton lost his grip on the grillwork and fell to one knee. He

"Peter!" she shouted. "Peter, where are you?"

She looked inside the Volvo and saw her small suitcase and Peter's on the backseat. She checked and saw the car keys were in the ignition. She got in behind the wheel, placed the jewel box on the seat next to her, and started the motor. She backed out of the garage and then saw it was impossible to attempt to leave by the front gate. She reversed the car and nosed it around the garage to the small road leading to the back exit. She was seen by a federal man, who fired one shot over the Volvo. Horace X. at first thought the shot was directed at him and swerved the motorcycle almost dislodging Irving the Gorilla. Then he saw the Volvo disappearing behind the garage, and Irving jabbed him frantically. Irving recognized the Volvo. Horace X. gunned his motor and took off in hot pursuit.

In her private chapel, Chloe Jupiter, with her faithful housekeeper Louella, knelt on pink heart-shaped cushions and prayed. Candles were lit and sent flickering shadows across her sad, lovely face.

"Uh want yuh tuh have mercy on muh niece, Viola Fairbanks, who has come tuh yuh for the rest and peace she has earned. Viola was a good kid but had no mother tuh guide her. Her mother was a immoral puhson what got thrown outta Pittsburgh for corruptin' miners. But on her deathbed, uh promised tuh do muh best for Viola. Muh best wasn't good enough." Louella sobbed softly and shook her head from side to side. How often, until Chloe had discovered her son rioting on television, had she feared the possibility of mourning his death. Even now, while praying for the safekeeping of Viola's soul, her mind dwelled on the possible danger he faced at Hagar's castle. "Punish me as yuh see fit, Lord," continued Chloe, "but grant me one favor before yuh pernt yuh finger. Deliver into muh hands Hagar Holt Simon. Ahhhhhh-*men*."

Norton had been dragged by Sparks up the stone staircase

11

Boyd Gross and the plainclothesman took the stone steps leading to the rampart two at a time. Boyd was the first to arrive at the top and saw Ira Sparks gripping Norton's ankles and Norton's arms flailing helplessly. Behind him Gross heard the plainclothesman ejaculate an astonished expletive, and the two of them lunged at Sparks. Sparks released his grip on Norton's ankles, and the hapless young man started to fall. Gross left Sparks to the plainclothesman and leapt for Norton, securing a good grip on his trouser waist and jacket. Sparks fought like a wild animal, and his stunned opponent was no match for him. He was too bewildered by the rush of events. Had Sparks been trying to rescue the guy or kill him? Sparks unleashed a powerful blow to his midriff that sent him reeling against Gross. Gross let out a yell as he almost lost his grip on Norton. Norton let out a yell as he felt himself slipping again. And Sparks disappeared down the stone steps. The plainclothesman got to his feet clutching his midriff, while fleetingly entertaining the thought of demanding a transfer to another precinct, then responded to Gross's cries for assistance. Together, they pulled Norton to safety.

herself away from the door, whimpering. She heard a second shot from the bedroom and screamed.

In the bedroom, Sparks clutched his bleeding right shoulder, his revolver having fallen to the floor. The plainclothesman stood trembling in the doorway, his gun aimed at his superior. Boyd Gross and Norton arrived and pushed their way past the man. They heard Sparks say in an ugly voice to the plainclothesman, "McCarthy, I'm gonna bust you for this!"

Hagar Simon knew her heart couldn't take much more of this. She was zig-zagging the Volvo around the rear of the castle grounds, constantly cut off from the escape by Horace X.'s deft manipulations of his motorcycle. She crashed into a statue of a winged Mercury, amputating his outstretched leg and then ricocheted into and castrated the statue of Jupiter. The pink bus was parked at a safe distance waiting for the motorized game of cat and mouse to end. Most of the passengers had disembarked to see if they were needed inside the castle. Hagar cursed aloud the name of her defected paramour, the chauffeur.

The chauffeur was on the front lawn, strolling arm in arm with the agent whose full-length mirror at home reassured him daily he was every bit as beautiful as Mark Spitz. The chauffeur was telling the agent, "After I left the Pasadena Playhouse, I tested at Metro, and then I got the lead in a low budget porno movie called *Show It Hard*. Then I was up for this jockey-short commercial, but I lost it to a friend of the director, so you know how it is. I had to take this job chauffeuring for Mrs. Simon. Well, you know how it is with these oversexed old bags . . ."

"I most certainly do," sympathized the agent, as he clucked his tongue, disengaged his arm, and patted the chauffeur tenderly on his back side, "and I think you have the makings of a big, *big* star."

The plainclothesman, who had been sent by Boyd Gross to

crouched down, reached for the handle of the door on the passenger side, and wrenched it open. He nimbly swung himself over and into the car next to Hagar. He switched off the ignition, pulled out the keys, and flung them out the door. Then he folded his arms and glared at Hagar with a snarling severity. Hagar shrieked, clutched her heart, and fainted. Horace X. opened the door on her side, lifted Hagar in his arms, and carried her to the pink bus. Irving the Gorilla took Hagar's jewel case and followed Horace X. and his burden to the bus. Horace X. returned to his motorcycle, set it erect, climbed on, and gunned his motor. He led the way to the front gate and back to Chloe Jupiter's house.

By now, most of the innocent guests had been cleared and had departed, after giving their names and addresses. Burton Hartley and Miklos Czardi were among those detained, along with some two dozen hoodlums and gangsters rounded up by the secret service men and the police. Hartley and Czardi were on the front lawn, Czardi protesting vociferously and demanding the right to phone the Hungarian embassy. Hartley espied Horace X. on his motorcycle followed by the pink bus, in which he saw the limp Hagar nestling in the arms of Irving the Gorilla. He advised a secret service man to relay this information to Norton Valentine.

Ira Sparks was stoically silent as he was led down the stairs past the dismantled suits of armor. The once stately interior of the castle now looked as though it had been raped, stripped, and pillaged by hordes of invading Tartars. Lila Frank was being assisted down the grand stairway, limping with the lack of one sandal, clutching her hip where the bullet had grazed it, by a very impressed Abe Grafton. He couldn't wait to tell his wife and his girl friend that he had spent part of the evening with the celebrated columnist.

Norton was told that Hagar had been taken to Chloe Jupiter's house and looked exasperated. And then it suddenly came back to him. Marti and Viola! What had become of

"You look as though you could use a doctor yourself," Gross said to Norton.

"I'll be okay," replied Norton, as he saw McCarthy hurrying toward them.

Earlier, while Norton had been offering Lila another chance at a deal, Marti Leigh lay in a state of semidelirium in a private room of the hospital. Outside in the corridor, a policeman guarded the door to her room. In Marti's room, a handsome young intern and a placid black nurse adjusted the weights that held her plaster-casted legs suspended from canvas-bottomed pulleys. Her face and both her hands were heavily bandaged. Detective Hank Rosen had been called back to duty and now anxiously waited for Marti to regain consciousness and give him a statement.

"The sky is falling, the sky is falling," mumbled Marti. Rosen didn't think it was worth making a note of that.

"Nortie . . . hurry, Nortie," continued Marti, and Rosen glanced at the intern, who shrugged.

"What's her chances?" Rosen asked the intern.

"It's anybody's guess," said the intern glumly. "I've seen some pull out of worse than this. I've seen others succumb to a simple fracture. It's the shock that does it."

"Shocking . . . very shocking," mumbled Marti.

Rosen turned to the nurse. "Say something to her."

"Like what?"

"I don't know. Anything. We've got to try to bring her around."

"Let me try," said the intern. He bent over Marti and spoke gently, "Miss Leigh . . . Miss Leigh . . . you're safe. You're alive. You're in the hospital, and you're being taken care of. Do you hear me, Miss Leigh?"

"Ummmm." Marti licked her lips and then groaned.

"Miss Leigh . . . this is Doctor Frisby . . . Lawrence Frisby . . ."

Marti groaned again and then slowly her eyes began to

subject. But when we get to Chloe Jupiter's, I think it'll all come out in the wash. Back there in Hagar's suite, that wasn't Lila Frank he thought he was shooting at. He was gunning for Hagar Simon. I think you can take it from there, if you start working backward."

"Ira's shoulder should be attended to."

"I don't give a damn if he bleeds to death! I hate that animal. He's not good enough to be called *pig*." Norton had wrenched open the door to the squad car and was staring directly at Ira Sparks. He was chagrined to see the man was in tears.

Burton Hartley was working overtime, currying favor with the detectives in the squad car transporting him and Miklos Czardi to central headquarters. Czardi was wondering how much he might get for his life story from *Esquire* if he got May Mann to ghost it. Hartley was telling the officers where to find Tom Gucci and Vince Hayes. There was a beatific expression on his face as he spoke. Burton Hartley felt he had found peace at last.

Back at the castle in the wreckage of the grounds at the rear, the septuagenarian Margot was leading her young Latin lover Manuel along a path strewn with shattered pieces of statuary and broken turf. She held tightly to his arm as she looked around her, like a dowager empress examining the ruins of a fallen empire. "You'll never see the likes of this again, Manuel," she cackled. "It's the last dinosaur. I caught that sly glance, you wicked thing. I'm the last pterodactyl. But all this," she waved a feeble hand in the direction of the castle, "will soon be razed and carted away. It was the last majestic symbol of old Hollywood. They'll subdivide this land and build dreadful little ranch type houses and destroy every trace of dear Isaac Simon's dream. Poor Isaac. Another Pygmalion destroyed by his Galatea. Did I ever tell you he was my first lover?" Manuel shook his head no as he stared at the castle and shivered. It was enshrouded with fog, and in before uh'm forgiven for muh sins of omission. Uh shoulda known the party was over when Norton came around tuh see me. Uh shoulda spilled the works 'n' saved Viola's life."

Horace X. said, "You couldn't have foreseen any of this."

"Uh know uh couldn't!" stormed Chloe. "Uh shoulda had the sense tuh consult Carroll Righter."

Irving the Gorilla heard the squad cars coming up the drive and set up a racket. Chloe sauntered to a front window and pulled back the ermine drapes. She saw Norton and the other detectives pouring out of the two cars with Ira Sparks and Lila Frank. "Ummmmm," murmured Chloe eyeing the detectives, "fresh men." She left the window and sauntered back to the sofa. "Horace X., we got uninvited company. Yuh better let 'em in. Uh don't mind an audience when uh tell Hagar what uh think of her."

"She's coming to," said Louella.

"Tuh what?" snapped Chloe. Irving the Gorilla was jumping up and down and chattering with excitement. "Irvin'! Settle down 'n' stop behavin' like uh ape." Irving the Gorilla slunk to the bar, hoisted himself on an ermine covered stool, and crossed his legs. He found a swizzle stick and rolled it back and forth between thumb and index finger. "That's better, Irvin'," said Chloe. "Yuh look suave. Yuh look like the late Adolphe Menjou."

Norton entered followed by Boyd Gross. Two detectives had a tight grip on each of Ira Sparks' arms, and he was wincing with pain. Lila Frank entered between another pair of detectives, one hand on her bruised hip.

Chloe glowered at Lila. "Yuh tryin' tuh imitate me, Lila?"

"No," growled Lila, "I got shot in the ass."

"Ummmm . . . uh'm shuah it ain't the first time. Hullo, Norton, yuh look like yuh been in a cement mixer. Horace X., uh think these gents could use a drink." She watched Ira Sparks lower himself onto a chair. She asked Norton, "What's with the detective man, Norton? He looks more like a prisoner."

Norton was staring at Hagar, watching the color come back

equipped with every modern convenience exceptin' compu-
ters. Irvin'! Go tuh muh room 'n' get muh heart-shaped tape
recorder." She said over her shoulder to Norton, "Uh had it
made especially for me in Japan." She looked at Ira Sparks's
injured shoulder. "Louella, uh think the detective man over
theah could use some first aid. Yuh can apply yuh second aid
to Miss Frank's left rear bumper."

Irving the gorilla returned with the tape recorder, and
Boyd Gross set it up on the heart-shaped coffee table.
"There's a fresh long-playin' tape in it," Chloe told Norton.
"Uh was gonna rehearse muh lines for a show uh'm gonna do
in Chicago. It's called *Mother Courage.*"

Norton found a smile at last. "You're going to do Brecht?"

"No, he'd dead. Uh'm just gonna do his play. Uh'm gettin'
the Sondheim kid tuh write me some songs, 'n' of course uh'll
be playin' the thing for laughs." She smiled at Boyd Gross.
"Uh see yuh got mechanical fingers. Norton, since uh'm the
star of this place, uh always get top billin'. So uh'm gonna
begin and speak muh piece first. Horace X., give Hagar
Simon some spirits tuh sip on." She smiled at Hagar with
irony. "Yuh lucky uh don't stock hemlock."

"I'm not well," muttered Hagar weakly, "I'm not well. I
must have a doctor. My heart . . . please understand . . .
I've had three attacks today . . . please somebody . . .
please . . ."

Boyd instructed one of the detectives to phone for an
ambulance. Chloe started the tape recorder.

"This begins a long time ago, Norton, long befoah a lot of
yuh was born. But it helps explain the events leadin' up tuh
the tragedies. Irvin', bring me a glass of muh mineral water."
She folded her arms and began pacing back and forth. She
saw an anxious look on Norton's face. "Don't worry about
muh walkin' back 'n' forth. This tape recorder picks up yuh
voice from a hundred yards or more. It's like the stuff Hagar
got placed all over the castle. Uh'm shuah you found them.
Well, Norton, uh'm shuah yuh heard of Salvatore Gucci, 'n'
so yuh heard of his eldest son Cristo."

into the castle and do the job for him Hagar's been doin'. Well y'know, Norton, uh'm a very loyal person. B'cause of muh religious beliefs, uh don't hold with nothin' immoral, illegal or illicit. But I owe the Gucci family. They put me where uh am t'day. Uh tell 'em they can have the castle, but they'll have tuh put someone else in tuh run it for them.

"Well, by this time, Gucci has quietly bought in tuh television 'n' radio 'n' films 'n' yeah, newspapers and some big newspaper syndicates. They need someone they can trust out here, so they create a celebrity. Right, Lila?"

Lila was staring at Chloe, while playing pat-a-cake with her fingers. "You tell it the way you know it, Chloe," said Lila huskily with a trace of venom. "This is your big scene. Make the most of it. It'll be your last."

Chloe replied icily, "Uh would'n' give yuh odds on that threat. Well, anyway, Norton, it's right about this time uh read that Cristo's been murdered on his own front lawn. Half his head shot away. Uh'll tell yuh why. He didn't want the old man back here. The old man's gettin' senile. He's crazy."

"He's not!" Irving the Gorilla pulled Lila back into the chair.

"It's like a Greek tragedy what happened tuh Cristo. His own kids, his own flesh 'n' blood, schemed tuh erase him. Because old Salvatore promised them power and money. He said he'd make 'em bigger than royalty. So Cristo's own son kills him and then comes West where his sister looks after him."

She paused dramatically and sauntered over to Lila. "The son what did the killin' is Tom Gucci. His sister is sittin' right here. Camille Gucci."

"Putana!"

"Whatever that is, honey, don't use too much garlic. So anyway, there's Hagar over here scratchin' at muh door back then, askin' for help. So uh turns her over to Camille or Lila or whatever yuh wanna call her. She's the bag woman for the old man."

Norton said to Lila, "Which explains the trips to Europe."

12

Ira Sparks removed his jacket. Louella had cut away his shirt with a scissors and was applying medication to his bullet wound. Now he brusquely shoved her away and leaned forward with his hands clutching his knees. "You were running away without me, Hagar. Why were you running away without me?"

Norton didn't recognize his voice. It was small and weak and sounded like the mock imitation of a child. For a wild moment Norton looked around the room to see if anyone was a ventriloquist throwing their voice.

"Why, Hagar? *Why?*"

Hagar pulled herself to a sitting position. "Because I loathed you. I loathed your touch, your slobbering kisses, your pathetic attempts at masculinity in the bedroom."

It took two men to restrain Sparks. He shrieked and cursed and then embarrassed them all by breaking into infantile sobs. Hagar's voice rose above the cacophony he was creating, as she looked directly at Norton.

"And I hated him for murdering Clay Stopley. My deal promised me no murder! I said that to him up on the began beating him mercilessly. I tried to pull Ira away, and Mr. Stopley fled up the stairs to the rampart. Ira pushed me aside . . . *quite* brutally, I might add . . . and chased him up there. I followed. I saw Ira kill him. With the help of some of my men, Ira took the body to Griffith Park. Ira will have to tell you the rest. I only know what I read in the papers."

Sparks had calmed down and was blowing his nose in his bandanna handkerchief. Irving the Gorilla regarded him with distaste.

"I hate your guts, Mr. Valentine."

"I know that, Ira."

"I hated Stopley for ignoring me the way he did. And I hated you for going out of your way to make me feel needed. You think I didn't know you had more respect for this shit!" He gestured toward Boyd Gross, who stared at the floor. "Hagar and me were going away together. She promised me that. I got a desk drawer filled with travel folders. We were lovers before she married Simon. When I was still a cop assigned to guard the stage door entrance at the arena. I mean . . ." his hands were outstretched with bewilderment, ". . . for years I stuck by her. I gave her money when she was broke. Then when she told me about fronting for the Gucci bunch and that, when she had her new pile made, we'd go away together . . . make a life together . . . I . . . I . . ."

"Sold yourself for a mess of pottage."

Sparks's eyes narrowed. "Well, why not, Mr. Valentine? Why not? It's a better reward than a gold watch and a slap on the back and a crappy pension that wouldn't feed a cage full of pigeons." He stared at his hands as though they were a surprise gift and then let them dangle as he slumped in his chair. "I was dumb. I was very dumb. I should have tossed Stopley's body in the drink for the fish to feast on. But I was in a panic, I guess. So I stripped his pockets and bashed his face in with a rock and took the rock and his wallet and everything else I found back to my apartment. Then I remembered Karen Frost. Hagar had told me she was in love

"Yeah. Then I forced the dissolved sleeping pills into her mouth while she was gasping for air."

Chloe crossed herself. "Even now uh'm askin' God tuh show yuh some mercy. If it was up tuh me, uh wouldn't."

Norton waved her to be quiet. "Tell us how you went after the girls."

"I went after Marti Leigh. I didn't know the Fairbanks kid would be with her." He said with irony, "Some days even I run lucky. I didn't want to use my own car. In case I slipped up, my license plates might be seen and traced. I had the keys to Frost's red Toyota." Norton couldn't resist an I-told-you-so look at Boyd Gross. Gross looked as though he had just heard a filthy epithet directed at the Pope. He was listening to Ira Sparks with dismay, disgust and disappointment. He was thinking of this black mark against his department.

"I parked my car a block away from Frost's place and took her car and drove out to Malibu. I got there just as I saw Leigh and the Fairbanks kid driving off in Leigh's yellow Chrysler convertible. Do I have to tell you the rest? I forced them off the road. I killed them."

"Marti Leigh's still alive," Norton said with some difficulty. "When Boyd heard you making the all-points alert for the girls, he thought he heard you mentioning the make and color of the car."

"Yeah, I started to. Then I caught myself. Just once I used my effing brains! Just that once!"

The police ambulance had arrived, and Horace X. went to the door. The phone rang, and Louella answered it. "Mr. Boyd Gross?" Gross crossed to her and took the phone. It was McCarthy on the other end. "Thanks, McCarthy. Norton guessed right on the Toyota." Norton tried not to look as though a laurel wreath had been placed on his head. "What was that, McCarthy?" Gross had a look of surprise. "Well, that's a pleasant bonus. Hey, Norton. The boys have rounded up Gucci and Hayes." Lila whispered a four-letter word. "They were tipped by our new friend Burton Hartley. He

"Both."

"All wrapped up."

"Tell me about it. Fast. I feel myself slipping away."

He recapped the evening's events for her swiftly. She had no special reaction when he named Ira Sparks as the murderer. She merely said, "The son of a bitch."

"Let's leave him to heaven."

"That's not where he's going."

And she was asleep. Norton left the room. He returned to the hotel, opened the sliding doors to the swimming pool, and then mixed himself a drink. He dialed his office on the turquoise phone and spent almost an hour reciting a meticulously detailed report. He was surprised he didn't fall asleep in the middle of it. After he hung up, he stripped off what was left of his clothes and took a hot shower. After toweling himself and putting on a robe, he returned to the living room and found Boyd Gross sitting with a drink in his hand.

"I hope I didn't frighten the hell out of you," said Gross. "I came out to the pool to see if there was a light on in your room. I saw the doors were open. If you're too tired to talk, I'll go away. But I won't sleep a wink tonight. I won't sleep any, thinking about Ira."

"Sure, old buddy. I'm not in the least bit tired," he lied. He poured himself a fresh drink and then sat opposite Gross. Norton had wanted to talk all night, too. He wanted to talk to Marti and ask her to marry him again. He had wanted to talk to her about perhaps leaving the service and going away together to start a new life. But he also knew it was a pipe dream. He knew he wouldn't quit his job, and he knew Marti would reject him. He had thought it out driving back from Hagar's castle after picking up the Renault. He sat watching Boyd Gross staring out at the pool, probably trying to find the words he wanted to say or a reason for saying them. He settled back in his seat and waited.